Beyond the
Galilee

Isaac Stenson

Order this book online at www.trafford.com
or email orders@trafford.com

Most Trafford titles are also available at major online book retailers.

Print information available on the last page.

ISBN: 978-1-6987-1616-9 (sc)
ISBN: 978-1-6987-1617-6 (e)

Library of Congress Control Number: 2023924229

Trafford rev. 12/28/2023

 www.trafford.com

North America & international
toll-free: 844-688-6899 (USA & Canada)
fax: 812 355 4082

Contents

Forward

By Gil Shapiro

The current Israeli-Hamas conflict, as well as millennia of volatility in the Middle East, has been caused by, at its core, religious belief.

In this tiny parcel of land that each group claims as its own, Christians, Muslims, and Jews have been at each other's throats for centuries for no other reason than their conflicting subjective "truths" about who created the universe. Indeed, their respective scriptures have encouraged bloodshed as the preferred means for asserting dominance, resolving disputes, and settling scores.

We must stop kidding ourselves that these religions promote tolerance, mutual respect, peace, and love. To those who question or reject this observation, I suggest a critical analysis of their respective holy texts. Pay close attention to the intolerance, disrespect, violence, and hatred directed towards non-believers. It becomes obvious that faith-based dogmas, above all else, have instigated and perpetuated these endless hostilities.

To wit: A Pew Research poll affirmed that most Muslims favor living in theocracies governed by Sharia, the moral and religious law of Islam.

Similarly, Israel's government is now guided by ultra-Orthodox religious and ultra-nationalist parties, and the West Bank is now "occupied" by hundreds of thousands of Jewish zealots.

Given this reality, it is no wonder that political negotiations, economic incentives, military threats, and initiatives to democratize Muslim cultures have never brought peace to the area.

Such factors make a two-state solution along with the hopes for a lasting peaceful co-existence, impossible.

With both sides firmly entrenched in their non-negotiable religious claims to the land, why do we waste time pursuing *guaranteed-to-fail* attempts to bring tranquility to the region?

The futile Israeli-Palestinian peace process must end. Both parties should concede that no workable solutions are possible.

My recommendation is that Israelis, individually or as a nation, leave the Middle East.

Why? Because remaining on this land, with no hope for a peaceful future, dooms them to living life on a perpetual war footing while being subject to inevitable decimation by a probable massive missile, chemical or nuclear attack. Indeed, Israeli defenses against such eventualities are wholly untested. And the threat of an Israeli nuclear retaliation is no deterrent to an enemy who relishes death in the pursuit of Jihad and of no value to an Israeli population that has just been annihilated.

Imagine you, your family, and friends lived in a community where you all had roots and every right to be…, but were surrounded and significantly outnumbered by neighbors who wanted to murder you. Would you stay or encourage your family and friends to live in such a dysfunctional and dangerous place? No way! Individuals who love themselves and their families would move. Only by leaving the Middle East will Israelis have a chance to lead calm and productive lives. This should not be interpreted as a capitulation to an enemy but rather as an affirmation of rationality and common sense.

Indeed, political, religious, legal, and emotional arguments against relocation pale when considering the terrible alternatives for remaining there.

Israelis who declare, "We must honor our post-Holocaust pledge, 'Never Again,' and continually fight and die for our land," are misguided. As a person of Jewish lineage, I urge Zionist zealots to reinterpret "Never Again" as a commitment to do whatever it takes to achieve a sane existence for themselves and future generations.

The United States should help make that happen if for one selfish reason: We have committed American lives and money to a nation that may draw us into nuclear conflict. We must extricate ourselves from this potentially catastrophic scenario.

Israelis have two choices for survival: to leave individually and settle elsewhere (which has always been an option); or to leave as a nation and establish a "New Israel" elsewhere in the world.

Both choices are obviously problematic: Because a critical mass of able-bodied citizens is required to defend the country, a major exodus of Israelis would be suicidal for the state. If Israelis decide, perhaps by national referendum, to seek a new homeland, where will they go? (Should America allow for a "New Israel" here?)

In 1939, there were 17 million Jews in the world; by 1945, at the end of Hitler's savagery in World War II, only 11 million remained. Today, Jews number about 17 million, with about 7 million in Israel. As a second Holocaust is likely, it is notable that the post-war Jewish population has just now reached its pre-war numbers.

Let's remember that Muslim extremists - --as the Nazis did --- have given Jews ample and unequivocal warnings of their genocidal intentions.

It is political and moral insanity to continue peace negotiations when it is theological lunacy, on both sides, that foments the hostilities. Reason has never and will never solve these intractable conflicts.

Individually or as a nation, Israelis must decide which they value more: religion and land or people and peace.

*Gil Shapiro lives in Oro Valley. He was the spokesperson for Freethought Arizona from 2005 to 2016. Contact him at: gdsh**apiro@** **comcast.net***

Prologue Vasilishok

At 04:45 on 22 June 1941, four million German soldiers, reinforced by Italian, Romanian and other Axis troops, burst over the borders and stormed into the Soviet Union, including the Belarus Soviet Socialist Republic. The Germans forces overcame all opposition that the Soviets and their allies could muster. The *Panzer* forces encircled hundreds of thousands of Soviet troops in huge pockets. The infantry divisions defeated the Soviets and their allies killing many and taking many prisoners. The panzers continued rolling, executing perfectly the *Blitzkrieg* doctrine.

It was March 31, 1941, when Dinah Rosenbeg answerd the door to her home in Vasisilshok. Reuvun Greenberg was at the door.

"Where is Schlomo? He asked. "He must come down to the city council for a meeting. The Germans have just sealed off Krakow and forced the Jews into a Ghetto. The council is attempting to get more news to decide what we are to do next."

"I will tell him." Dinah replied.

"Hurry! Don't tary!" Reuven said as he turned away for another home to inform.

Schlomo Rosenberg left his home and rapidly walked toward Rabbi Cohen's home where he knew the shtetil's prominent citizens would be.

When he knocked on the door the Rabbi's wife answered and invited him in. She led him to the large study where several men were gathered in a heated discussion.

"What is happening?" Schlomo asked.

"We have just received news that the Germans have portioned off Krakow and established a ghetto where they are forcing all the Jews to live. We know that bad times are coming for Jews everywhere the Germans come." Rabbi Cohen answered.

"How far is Krakow from Vasilishok?" Yshak Finkel asked.

"It's seven hundred and fifty kilometers." Garz, one of the water carriers answered.

"What's next? What are we to do?" Schlomo asked addressing his question to the group.

There was a pause.

"We must answer the Soviets request for more men to join their forces. They're requesting two hundred more volunteers." Rabbi Cohen answered.

"Thank you." Schlomo answered. "I have pressing matters at home. I must leave now but I will stay in touch."

When Schlomo arrived home, he informed his wife what was happening.

"What do we do now?" She asked, distraught.

"I am going to Lida where there is a communications office to send a cable to my brother in the United States. It is only thirty kilometers from Vasilishok. I will hire Peter Grodinski the Polish driver to take me. Stay home, lock the doors and don't go anywhere until I return."

He returned an hour later. On the way home he noticed that the lights to Rabbi Cohens's house were out.

I'll find out tomorrow what they decided he thought to himself. He had received several letters from his brother Heinrich Rosenberg begging him to leave while he could and to come to America. He would send him the funds and the paperwork to complete. All he had to do was to make his way to the nearest free city with an American embassy to receive his visa.

The words of his brother's admonition were on his mind:

You can be certain that the Germans will break their nonagression pact with the Soviet Union and invade Russia as soon as they can. They will come to your area on their way to the farmlands of Ukraine to ensure their food supply. When they come, they will bring special units to kill the Jews and other undesirable people.

His brother had fled the shtetil for the United States immediately after they had received word of Kristallnacht. His brother, a schoolteacher, was a Melamed who had purchased and read a copy of Hitler's Mein Kampf.

It is no secret what Hitler has in mind for the Jews he had pleaded. Come, while you still can!

The words of his brother repeated themselves in his mind.

When he entered the house, he told Dinah: "Please, let us get rest tonight. Tomorrow we will begin to pack to leave to the United States.

22 June 1941

The pact was terminated on 22 June 1941, when Germany launched Operation Barbarossa and invaded the Soviet Union, in pursuit of the ideological goal of Lebensraum. The Anglo-Soviet Agreement succeeded it.

17 September 1939 – two weeks after the outbreak of World War Two, the Red Army moved into West Belarus. June 1941 – the start of the Great Patriotic War in Belarus. June-July 1941 – resistance in Brest against German invaders lasted 6 weeks. The city was occupied until Soviet troops liberated it in 1944.

Introduction

Well, I don't believe that heaven waits
for only those who congregate, I like to think of God as love
He's down below, he's up above.[1]

I am compelled to write this historical fiction. I believe I am challenged because the discovery of documents which describe the early days of Christianity point to a time of competeing interests. Those who called themseves Christians were struggling to understand the words and actions of those who had proceded them. There was no written dogma in those early years. The documents which I refer to in this work existed prior to the Church's choice to accept the decision of the Emperor Constantine to unite his empire under what would become the Pauline form of Christianity. I believe that divine revelation throught the Holy Spirit comes to all peoples. I may not change my religious beliefs as a result of these early documents but the fact that they exist should be recognised. To quote the Prelate of Antiochus in this tale, the Emperor is no more qualified to determine what brand of Christianity is true than anyone else. History has certainly proven he was qualified to decide which brand of Christianity he would choose to unite his empire.

I understand that many of those who believe in Christianity are not overly concerned with what these documents offer to give us: an understanding of the early church. There are those who are seeking to grasp a deeper understanding of the faith that they were raised in. For those who seek a greater understanding of early Christianity, the documents alluded to in this story have certainly been vetted and are

---

[1]   Williams, Don *I Believe in You*, Some Broken Hearts Never Mend, 1977

almost certainly genuine. Read them, understand them and the history during which they were written, then decide for yourself.

The words that the Creator created Heaven and Earth must mean more than this small planet in one small corner of the universe. It is a metaphor for all of creation.

CHAPTER ONE

———〜〜◦◦❀❀◦◦〜〜———

Elisheva

West to Arizona

E lisheva laid her coffee on the table and picked up her cell phone. "Mother", she said, "this looks ideal. It's a small Airbnb in Tucson located not far from the University of Arizona. It is in a quiet neighborhood in the back of a residence. I'm going to call and see if I can reserve it for two weeks."

"OK," her mother replied. "Don't forget we're going to grandmother's house for dinner tonight at six."

"I won't. Hopefully, I'll be able to tell them my itinerary and plans."

After a few minutes on the telephone with the Airbnb national office she terminated the call.

"Good news, Mom. I've got the reservations confirmed from October fifteenth through the twenty sixth. I'm going to call Jonah to let him know when I will arrive. I am really excited now that things are beginning to fall into place. The last time I spoke with Jonah he said that he was through with the conservation and was awaiting further instructions on what to do about the codex. Maybe tonight I'll be able to ask grandpa if he's heard anything."

They arrived at the Brownstone apartment in the Bronx where they were both reared and had lived with Elisheva's grandparents, her widowed mother, Esther Gurwitz's parents. They climbed the steps and rang the doorbell. They were greeted by Dinah Rosenberg, Esther's mother and Elisheva's grandmother.

1

"Come in! Come in! Sholem Aliekhem!" Dinah exclaimed, obviously delighted to see her daughter and granddaughter.

"Aliekhem shalom." Esther replied.

"Aliekhem shalom." Elisheva replied.

Dinah led her daughter and granddaughter into the living room where Schlomo sat in a stuffed recliner.

"Good evening, Grandpa!" Elisheva said as she quickly went to her grandfather and kissed him on the cheek and took his hand in hers.

"Good evening, child." Schlomo replied. "What a blessing you are to an old man."

"Grandpa! You're not old! Age is just a number." Elisheva said as she sat down on the settee across from her grandfather.

"Good evening, Father." Esther remarked as she kissed him on the cheek. She sat next to her daughter and the two of them looked expectantly at Schlomo.

"Well, let's not delay any longer. Jonah called Chief Rabbi Mendelsohn today to advise him that his work conserving and refurbishing both the scroll and the codex is now complete. He asked that Rabbi Lipschitz and an escort return to Tucson to take possession of the documents. He also advised that he would give two extremely accurate copies of the both the scroll and the codex to Elisheva.

"Rabbi Lipschitz will be flying down from Philadelphia to meet Frederick Longwill here. He will accompany him to Tucson to take possession of both documents and return them to me. I have arranged to have a strong safe installed here in our apartment until we complete the transfer of the scroll from us to the synagogue.

"Now, have you made reservations to leave for Tucson, Elisheva?"

"Yes, Grandpa. I have found an ideal Airbnb in Tucson in a quiet neighborhood within walking distance of the University. I will be leaving in a week. I have already reserved the Airbnb and will finalize my airline reservations tonight."

"We will pray that you have a safe journey to Tucson and back." Dinah said.

CHAPTER TWO

—‿‿◦e᷎ᷠ◦᷎ᷠe◦᷎◦‿‿—

Santiago

El amor entra por los ojos.
(Love enters through the eyes)
Mexican proverb

Santiago Valencia pulled up to the small home on Lee Street. He placed the cardboard sunshade over the dashboard of his Ford Ranger pickup and called his grandmother on his cell phone.

When the woman on the other end of the call answered he told her: "Abuela, I'm here at the Airbnb and the renter has not yet arrived. I'll go inside and unlock the door and make sure the cleaning lady has everything ready. Also, since I just watered everything yesterday the plants and trees look in good shape. I'll use my air blower to blow any leaves and dust that may have accumulated since I was here yesterday."

"Good, Mijo," his grandmother answered. "If she arrives while you are still there let me know."

"I will, Abuela." He replied. "Goodbye."

"Goodbye." His grandmother replied.

Santiago had completed his tasks and was walking back to his truck when he saw a small Volkswagen Jetta parked on the street in front of his pickup. He waited to greet the driver. An attractive young woman who appeared to be his age came into view.

"Hello." He greeted her. "Are you looking for the Airbnb?"

"Yes. Are you the owner?" She replied.

"Oh, no. My grandmother is. I just help her out with keeping the outside watered and picked up. She asked me to unlock the door and ensure the place is ready for you."

"Is your grandmother, Angela Torres?" She asked.

"Yes. My name is Santiago, but everyone calls me Jaime. It looks like you're driving a rental car. My grandmother said you would be arriving at the airport today and renting a car before you arrived. Can I help you unload your luggage? By the way, what is your name?"

Elisheva did not immediately reply. She looked at him for just a few seconds. *He seems sincere and if he tries to do anything I can call his grandmother. Also, she reckoned, I could probably immobilize him pretty quickly if need be.*

"Elisheva, but everyone calles me Ellie. Yes, you would be a big help with the luggage. I know I'm supposed to park on the street, but do you think it would be OK if I were to back up the car in the driveway to unload my stuff?"

"Absolutely!" He answered. 'My grandmother also owns the rental in front of the Airbnb. The nice couple have lived there for some ten years and know that it is usual for someone with baggage to park there until they unload."

He walked with her to the driveway and waited until she backed the car up close to the parked car with his directions.

She opened the door and handed him a suitcase and a duffle bag which he took to the Airbnb. He opened the door and placed the items in the living room. Elisheva followed right behind him with a black canvas bag that Santiago recognized carried a laptop computer and probably the necessary items to go with it. After two more trips she returned to the Jetta and parked it on the street.

"Thank you for helping me." She told him with a smile.

"You're welcome." He replied. "If you need anything at all during your stay here just call my grandmother and she will see to it."

"Is this your full-time job?' She smiled. *He has beautiful brown eyes.*

"Oh, no." He told her. "I've just completed my two-year stint in the navy. I joined the reserves while I was at the U of A and just recently completed my two-year active-duty obligation."

"Interesting," she replied, "what did you do on active duty?"

"I was an Intelligence Specialist. Do you know anything about Navy ratings or job specialties."

"No. But I am certainly interested. Do you have time to sit for a few minutes before I start putting things away? I don't know much about the military, but I can assure you my family is deeply appreciative and grateful for what the US military did for us."

"Hmmm. Now you've got my interest! A Navy Intelligence Specialist, or *IS* in navy speak, is part of the navy's Information Warfare community. It was by combining the Photographic Intelligence Man, or *PT*, rating with the Yeoman, or *YN*, rating. After I completed Boot Camp, or Basic Training I took a semester off to attend and complete the "A" school at the Marine Technical Training Center at Dam Neck, Virginia."

"Is that a semester training class?"

That was thirteen weeks long. I received my degree in Electrical Engineering. Then I attended a thirteen week "C" school, again at Dam Neck, Virginia. I was then assigned to an amphibious Dock Landing Ship, the USS Wasp, LHD1. It carries a Marine Expeditionary Force, helicopters, amphibious landing craft and fighter aircraft, including the F35B."

"I'm impressed. Tell me: do women serve aboard ship?"

"Yes. There were women Operations Specialists, *OS* in navy speak, who served alongside me in the Combat Information Center, CIC, in navy terms. There are also women pilots and officers aboard ship."

"I didn't know that. It seems I might have missed something when I was searching for a career. Santiago, or can I call you Jaime, what are your plans for the future?"

"I'm not one hundred percent sure. I was toying with the idea of continuing on to get my masters in electrical engineering, but I am also considering taking some different courses to explore other fields besides engineering. However, I've been somewhat distracted doing some genealogy work. I found out that my Abuela, or grandmother, comes from a *crypto Jewish* background."

"Crypto Jew?" I am Jewish. But I have not heard the term Crypto Jew."

"That is someone who, in Spain during the Inquisition of 1492, was forced to convert to Catholicism, or face severe consequences, such as expulsion, or worse yet, torture and death by burning at the stake."

"Oh yes, the *New Christians* as they were referred to, were ostensibly Catholic."

"Yes, but they continued to practice their Jewish faith in secret, often at a great risk to themselves. Through concentrated research, I found out that my ancestors chose to leave Spain and travel to Bohemia, which at that time, in the year 1492, had a large and established Jewish population. Eventually, however, they immigrated to Mexico. They traveled as far as they could to get away from the Inquisition. Sadly, however, the practices continued with the Spanish conquistadors and clergy. There is much to their story. I just returned from a conference in El Paso sponsored by the Society for Crypto Jewish Studies. They peaked my interest and I've been thinking of traveling to Europe to find the places where my family lived during those times. They had to take surnames because the kings and princes at that time needed to keep track of their population for purposes of taxation and military service. My family chose the surname Valencia. Wow! I have been talking too much.

"Tell me, what brings you to Tucson? My grandmother said you were here to do some research and pick up some documents. That sounds pretty interesting to me."

"It seems like a coincidence! What you've told me is fascinating. As I said, I am also Jewish. My family is Orthodox and my grandparents managed to escape from their shtetl before the Germans captured the town where they lived."

"Oh, yes. So you would be an Ashkenazi Jew?"

"All this is so fascinating. I would love it if we could continue talking. But I am starving. I haven't eaten for hours. I was reading some of the literature on the Airbnb website and they had a write-up of some of the Mexican restaurants in Tucson. I have had some east coast Mexican food, but I'll wager the local cuisine is better."

"Great! I know a restaurant that you would like. I've got some time right now. Would you like to join me in one of my favorites?"

"I would love it. Then I can explain why I am here. Give a couple of minutes to unpack some of my things and at least temporarily put them away.

CHAPTER THREE

Tucson, Arizona, the Old Pueblo, South of
the Gila River in Baja Arizona

"OK, I'm ready." Elisheva said.

She locked the door to the Airbnb, which was also referred to as the "Casita". Santiago followed her as she walked to the Jetta and made sure the doors were locked. He opened the door to the Ford Ranger and helped her to adjust the seat.

"I like your pickup." She told him as she looked out the window. "Are you a hunter or cowboy?"

He laughed at her remark.

"No, but I do like to putz around in the desert and mountains here in southern Arizona. A lot of folks from other states seem to think that the desert doesn't have much to offer but there are many places here in Pima County in general and southern Arizona in particular that I, at least, find interesting."

It was her turn to laugh.

"Putzing around?" She asked. "Do you have any idea of the origin of that word."

"No, but you've got my interest. Tell me."

"Putz comes from Yiddish. It technically means to putter about. Which is probably what you meant. Like puttering about in the garden or something similar. But it also means, in Yiddish, a "penis.""

She looked at him with a smile and was surprised to see him blushing.

"Oh," he quietly replied with a sheepish grin, "I'll be more careful how I use that word. You speak Yiddish? I should have guessed since you are Jewish. Your family is from Eastern Europe. You should have a background in Yiddish. My family's background is Ladino, which is very similar to Spanish, in general, and Catalan, in particular. I learned both from my research and from attending the SCJS that there have been Jews in Spain, called Sepharad in Hebrew, since the Second Temple. Sephardic Jews to this day consider their history in Spain as a Golden Age, mostly under the rule of the Moors. One of the projects I was thinking about is learning Ladino, and maybe even Hebrew."

"Yes, and that is the essence of why I am in Tucson. That is also the reason I asked what your plans for the immediate future were."

"Wow." He uttered.

"What do you mean by that, Jaime?"

"You are definitely the most interesting woman I have ever met. I would certainly like to learn more about you."

"You've got a deal. Let's have a leisurely dinner in a reasonably quiet place and learn more about each other."

He drove to the El Vaquero Family Restaurant in downtown Tucson. After parking the Ranger across the street and putting his credit card into a machine, he received a parking ticket good for five hours. They walked across the street and entered the lobby where a young and pretty woman greeted them.

"Bienvenidos," she said. "How many tonight?"

"Es possible que tengamos un mesa para dos un poco privada, por favor?" He answered.

After they were seated and ordered dinner and wine, she asked him. "You speak Spanish?"

"You speak Yiddish? He said.

"Yes. I tell you what. After we're served, I'll tell you why I'm here and why I'm interested in your future plans. In the meantime, I like this restaurant with all the old photos of families. I assume that the greatest part of the photos is of Mexican or Mexican American families. Some of the black and white photos look very old."

"They are. If you're up to it, after we finish our dinner and conversation, we can take a brief walk around the neighborhood. I'll show you all the different types of homes that still exist here, although most have been restored to their original condition, at least on the exterior. The interiors are pretty up to speed with all the modern conveniences."

"I'd love to. I see they served two dishes of dip with corn chips. What's the difference?"

"One is usually a mild sauce, the other is more spicy. I usually don't try either one until I have something cold to drink. Since we have ice water on the table, try each one and see what you think."

She did as he recommended. The first bowl was delicious. The second bowl caused her to quickly reach for a glass of ice water.

"I know what you mean! That second one is obviously the spicy one. It is very tasty, but it actually burned my lips and kind of cleared my sinuses!"

Santiago laughed: "Well, I'm glad you at least found the spicy one tasty. It grows on you. You always have the option of mixing the two together."

The waiter placed the combination plate in front of Elisheva.

"This looks delicious. Let me see: this is the Spanish rice, these are the refried beans with cheese, this is obviously a taco, and these two smothered in sauce and covered with shredded lettuce are the enchiladas?" She asked.

"Yes. I basically have the same thing with the exception of my flat enchilada covered with only chili, and a green corn tamale, which I will share with you so you can get a taste of everything."

He then took his glass of wine and reached out to her: "Salud! A toast to what I hope is the beginning of a new friendship."

"Aleicheim Shalom!" She responded. I also hope we are beginning a new friendship."

They began to eat and after a few sips of wine Elisheva began to tell Santiago why she had come to Tucson.

"Jaime, I'll start from the beginning and try to include the essential bits of information that will explain to you why I'm here. If you have any questions, just ask and I will try to expand.

"I was born in the Bronx, which is part of New York City. It's one of the boroughs. My father's name was Morris Gurwitz. My mother's maiden name is Rosenberg. Unfortunately, I never had a chance to know my father well. He died when I was two years old. My father was an Ashkenazi Jew who died from something called late onset Tay-Sachs disease. Morris' parents were both murdered in Poland by the Germans and their Polish collaborators. He was rescued by a devout Catholic woman and was sent to a British displaced person's camp after the war. We later learned from his physicians that neither of his parents were affected but they were carriers of the gene that they unwittingly passed on to him.

"He was sent to live with an aunt and uncle in Brooklyn. He went to work at his uncle's jewelry store until he graduated from Thomas Jefferson High School. He graduated from the High School's honors program and received a scholarship to the University of Rhode Island in Kinston. That is where he met my mother. Both were working at a summer studies program in Rhode Island at the Touro Synagogue, which, by the way, is the oldest one in the United States.

"My mother, Esther Rosenberg is her maiden name, was reared in her parent's house, a brownstone apartment. After my father passed, both she and I went to live there. Are you familiar with a brownstone apartment?"

"No", he answered. "But I want to learn more about what they are."

"I'll show you photos later. Let me tell you about my grandparents. I love my grandparents. My grandmother's name is Dinah. My grandfather's name is Schlomo Rosenberg. They were born in a small village called a shtetl. The Vasilishok Shtetl. At the time it was located southwest of the large city, Vilne, Lithuania. At times it's also called Wilno, Poland. The boundaries of the countries in Europe, especially in eastern Europe, change with the different wars and alliances. Vasilishok was close to the border of what is now Poland, Lithuania and Belarus. It probably doesn't mean much to you now, but it will. Vasilishok is on the route that leads from Grodno to Vilna and from Lida to Schutchin. Schutchin is an administrative district in what is now Belarus. The Vasilishok Jews had lived for generations in the community and for a thousand years in Poland. During World War Two the Germans conquered the entire area and murdered all the Jews with the exception of only a handful that managed to escape. Fortunately, my grandparents were among the few that managed to get away. They left with only a few possessions. They escaped by paying a loyal Polish employee who owned an automobile a considerable amount of money to take them to the nearest city unconquered by the Germans and from there they made their way to Italy.

"From Italy they managed to get to the United States because my grandfather, Schlomo, has a brother in the United States who had fled the shtetl right after Kristallnacht in Germany. He saw the writing on the wall but couldn't convince Schlomo to do likewise.

"I'm going to go the lady's room. When I return, I will tell you why I've given you all this background."

Santiago stood up as she left. He sat down and pondered on what she had told him. There was a lot to digest, and he wanted to know what she meant when she said all this has been background. When she returned they finished their meal and after the table was cleared had another glass of wine.

"I mentioned earlier that my grandparents, the Rosenbergs, managed to escape with a few possessions. One of those possessions was a trunk which contained an old Sefer scroll. Do you have any idea what a Sefer scroll is?"

"Yes, but tell me anyway."

"A Sefer scroll is a handwritten copy of the Torah, or the first five books of Moses. It is always written by a pious scribe in the original Hebrew. The Sefer scroll had been in the Ark of the synagogue, the Vasilishok Schul. It had been especially prepared hundreds of years before to be placed in that Ark. At the beginning of the eastward sweep of the German Wehrmacht, the Rabbi had removed the Sefer scroll from the Ark and had taken it to my grandfather for safekeeping. My grandfather was a Melamed, which in Hebrew means Teacher. My grandfather promised the Rabbi that he would guard it with his life and that he would ensure it would find a sacred place where it could again be honored and read."

"Let me interrupt to ask a question. You said it had been in the Vasilishok Schul for hundreds of years. Doesn't schul mean school? I took two years of German and I believe the German word for school is *die Schule*."

"You are correct. Yiddish derives many of its words from German and schul in Yiddish means school. The Germans would not permit the Jews to build more synagogues than they thought they needed. They imposed a relatively heavy tax on synagogues. They permitted them to build as many schools as they could which were taxed at a much lower rate. So, every synagogue, which was also a place of learning, was referred to as a schul.

"The loyal Polish employee who had driven my grandparents to freedom asked them for a favor in return. He handed my grandfather a leather case which contained, in his words, an ancient sacred codex. The codex had been given to him by Father Belinski, the pastor of one of the oldest Catholic churches in the Shcutchin administrative district. The driver told my grandfather that he had attempted to convince Father Belinski to escape with him. The priest had refused and said his place was here with his parish. He did tell the driver that what he was given was a precious codex from ancient times and to guard it with his life. My grandfather accepted the codex and placed the leather case in the trunk alongside the Sefer scroll.

"My grandparents eventually settled in the Bronx and joined the Bronx Park Avenue Synagogue. Schlomo, or "MO" as he came to be called, opened up a hardware store where he was able to make a living and support his family, which, as I mentioned, included both my mother and me. Both my mother and I worked at the hardware store. I would work there on weekends and during summer break until I went to college. Both my grandparents remained active in the synagogue and after Schlomo retired they became even more active.

"There was a visit to the synagogue by an elderly Rabbi, Rabbi Levi Lipschitz, that had lived in a shtetl near the Vasilishok shtetl. My grandparents invited him to dinner. My mother and I were both there to meet this revered Rabbi who many in the congregation considered holy. I really enjoyed the evening, especially listening to the stories about the shtetl before the war and how life was then. There were many happy stories and laughter as well as the shared terror and sadness of the past and of loved ones who were murdered. During dessert my grandfather told the Rabbi that he was going to show him a treasured Sefer scroll that was their intention to donate to the synagogue. When my grandfather revealed the scroll to him the Rabbi was astounded. He admonished all of us not to get too close to the scroll because the humidity from our breath could damage it. He also told us to wear gloves and not to touch it. He asked my grandfather to repackage it as it had been. He then advised my grandfather that he knew of a conservator of Sefer scrolls. His name is Jonah Weisenberg and that he was currently working at the Center of Judaic Studies in the College of Social and Behavior Sciences at the University of Arizona. Jonah Weisenberg was the grandson of a man who did not survive the Holocaust. His grandfather had been a conservator as was his father who continued in the profession until he passed. Jonah had learned his trade from his father and also had worked with an experienced conservator in the Boston area.

"My grandfather unveiled the codex to Rabbi Lipschitz. When the Rabbi saw the codex he clutched his chest, sat down and asked for a glass of water. When he recovered from his apparent shock, he told us that the codex before us was much more ancient than the scroll. He estimated that the scroll was between three hundred to five hundred years old. He then told us that he believed the codex was much more ancient, at least two thousand years old!

"My grandfather complied with the Rabbi's instructions and repackaged the two documents as they had been. Rabbi Lipschitz met with the Rav Rashi, as he referred to him. The Rav Rashi is Chief Rabbi Mendelsohn of the Bronx Park Avenue Synagogue. Together they arranged for Rabbi Lipschitz to courier the two documents to Jonah Weisenberg at the University of Arizona accompanied by the Gabbai, or Treasurer, of the synagogue. His name is Frederick Longwill. They received a stipend for the endeavor and to defray any costs incurred by the conservator. When the Sefer Scroll was refurbished, it would be donated to the Bronx Park Avenue Synagogue as a gift from the Rosenberg family. What was to be done with the ancient code was to be determined after the conservation. Any questions, Jaime?"

"I feel that I should be taking notes. I am fascinated by what you've told me."

"I have told you quite a bit, but don't worry there is no quiz you have to pass and in any case, I can always answer any questions you might have. Let's take that walk you promised."

"You've got a deal. Let me pay and we'll get started."

CHAPTER FOUR

⸱⸱⸱⸱⸱⸱⸱⸱⸱⸱⸱⸱⸱⸱⸱⸱⸱⸱⸱⸱⸱⸱⸱⸱

Camina conmigo por el barrio
(Walk with me through the neighborhood)

After they left the restaurant, they walked north. She placed her arm inside his.

He began to tell her about the different houses and offices in the barrio.

"That house across the street is an old, whitewashed adobe. There is a young family that live there. Apparently, they are gardeners because you can't help but notice all the flowers and plants in the yard. This is a good example of pre-railroad Sonoran architecture when Tucson was still a part of Mexico. The one on this side of the street is post-railroad Sonoran which means that new building materials were available when Tucson was part of the United States."

A few minutes later they came to an intersection and paused.

"That building to the right across the intersection is transitional territorial. It is now a law office. Previous owners over the years have modernized the interior while maintaining the exterior which is required by the city historical zoning regulations in order to comply with federal historical designation. I was in that building during a sponsored tour of this area. It is fully equipped with internet access, a modern fire suppression system, a law library and some great paintings by local artists. I was very impressed."

"That's interesting. Just walking through this neighborhood makes me realize how Tucson looked in the past.

"Let me ask you a question," she said as they turned around and started walking towards the parking lot.

"Do you have a significant other? You don't have to answer if you don't want to. You may find me rather nosy."

"I don't mind. I have been seeing one girl in particular, a teacher. She recently left for a counselor's position in a Burbank, California school district. We correspond by email occasionally but I believe she is interested in another man, the father of one of her students. We don't correspond much anymore. And no, I don't mind you asking. That lets me ask about you. What about you, do you have a significant other?"

"Yes, I do. His name is David Finklestein. His family is from Brooklyn. He's doing pretty well as a banker in Manhattan where he lives. He was being considered for a vice president position when I last spoke with him. I would occasionally take the train to Manhattan and spend a couple of days with him. By the train I mean the subway of the MTA, the Metropolitan Transit Authority."

"I know about the MTA from the Kingston Trio song about a man that got stuck and couldn't afford to get off."

"You're not old enough to actually have heard that song by the Kingston Trio! You must like a wide variety of music."

"I do. It ranges from country, or at least what I would call *classical country*, to Mexican to even some opera."

"What's your favorite aria?"

"Nessun Dorma. Especially the one sung by Andrea Bocelli. But I also like the renditions by Pavarotti and others. But let me ask you since you've diverted my question about your significant other. If you would be spending time together in Manhattan, I would believe that you two were serious."

"Yes. You're correct. We have been dating for two years and I know he is about to propose to me. But I am not ready to commit to a marriage at this point in my life. This experience with the Sefer scroll and even the codex has given me a new purpose that I want to achieve before I settle down. One of the items I will pick up from Jonah Weisenberg when I meet him next week is a very good copy of both the scroll and the codex. I deeply desire to travel to that part of Belarus. The Vasilishok Shtetil used to be just across the border from Belarus in Lithuania. I desire to see what is left of it. I desire to actually walk the ground where is was before being destroyed. I have done research on it, and it is no longer standing. I know there is a Jewish graveyard nearby which had been overrun by weeds and grass for years. Many of the gravestones were taken and used for building materials. There was a Jewish historical society that traveled from the United States to Vasilishok and paid to have the graveyard cleaned and maintained. They hird a local contractor to build an iron fence around it. Many of the grave markers were lost but there are plaques where people are buried and historical markers with some of the original writing on the markers. To tell you the truth, Jaime, I have this deep yearning to actually see and walk the area of my grandparents. I'm not sure if the original synagogue is standing but if it is or isn't, I want to walk on the plot of ground where it was."

"What about a job. Are you currently working?"

"Yes. I have a job with a life insurance company, Middleton Life. I was recently promoted to Vice President of demographics in the Underwriting department which included a significant payraise. I have been able to save quite a bit. In addition, my grandparents, Dinah and Schlomo, have given both my mother and me a significant inheritance. My grandparents made some careful investments. Like many other immigrant Jews Schlomo joined a landsmanshaft, or mutual aid society in which he has received excellent investment advice. So, there you have it. I have revealed many of my personal secrets to you. We were complete strangers until today!"

"Don't worry. I would never say anything about you that you would not want me to say."

"OK, as long as we're in this tell all mood, what religion are you?"

"I was raised Catholic, but I never was as pious and devout as my grandmother. I have been doing a lot of research about my Jewish heritage. I have even come across what I consider compelling evidence that Christopher Columbus was a crypto Jew![2] Why? Does that make a difference to you."

"I honestly don't know. My family has sacrificed a lot just for being Jewish. I have one more question after we get back into your truck and head for the Airbnb. Are you able to travel? I intend to fly from Tucson back to New York and from New York to a city as close to Vasilishok as I can get. I did some preliminary checking and I think that Prague might be a good city from which to start."

"What a coincidnce! I've mentioned previously that I've been about traveling to Europe. How about if we travel together?"

"Yes that would be great!" She answered.

---

[2]   Eugene Sierras, The Way of Saint James; Journey to America (Bloomington, Indiana: Trafford publishing, 2019) xiv

After they arrived at the Airbnb she invited him in to sit and talked while she unpacked.

"I feel insecure going into an area I'm not familiar with tomorrow. I would love to have someone come with me to pick up these valuable copies tomorrow. I could probably find my way, but it would help to have someone who knows his way around. I know the University is within walking distance. I would not want to carry the documents with me, even though they are copies. I want to put them in my car where they won't be visible to anyone. If you could come with me I would gladly repay the favor by treating you to lunch"

"Yes, gladly. I will be here tomorrow to drive with you and show you where to park. What time is good for you?"

"You tell me."

"Great, I'll see you tomorrow at 9 a.m."

"Good night. Thank you, Jamie."

CHAPTER FIVE

⸺ ∿⌖◦⊙⟊⊙⌖◦∿ ⸺

Learn from the past. Explore new ways of thinking.
Jewish Studies gives you that opportunity.
(Motto of the Center for Judaic Studies, College of Social
and Behavioral Sciences, University of Arizona)

Santiago was able to quickly find a parking spot near their destination using his college student parking sticker which permitted students who have paid a fee to park on the campus itself and not on the nearest parking garage. From Speedway Boulevard he turned south on Park Avenue then East on First Street then north to Olive Street.

"That building ahead of us is Holtzclaw Hall. I can park here. We're only a short distance from the Judaic Center. It will be an easy walk." He told her.

"Great! I'm so anxious and not just a little bit nervous to go. Vamonos!" She replied as she exited the truck.

After a five-minute walk they entered the building and took the elevator to the fourth floor. As they entered Suite 420, they were greeted by a receptionist.

"Good morning. How can I help you."

"We're here to see Doctor Jonah Weisenberg." Elisheva answered.

"Oh. Yes. He's expecting you. Please follow me." She directed as she stood up. She paused in front of a door marked with Dr. Jonah Weisenberg's name and knocked.

"Yes, please come in, Rebecca." A man's voice said.

"Dr. Weisenberg, this is Elisheva." Rebecca introduced.

Jonah Weisenberg stood up and walked to them.

18

"Elisheva! Finally! I'm so pleased to have finally met you in person. Please come in and sit down. Who is your friend?" He asked returning to his desk.

"This is Santiago Valencia. He is a graduate from the Engineering College and is currently enrolled in some upper-level courses."

Jonah reached across the table and extended his hand to Santiago who shook his hand.

"Welcome Santiago. It's a pleasure to meet you."

"It's also my pleasure, Sir."

"Please sit down. I'm sure Elisheva is quite anxious to get started. Briefly let me bring you up to speed. Yesterday I spoke both with Rabbi Lipschitz and Frederick Longwill, as you know the Treasurer of the synagogue. They will be arriving here to take possession of both documents. I mentioned that we are very fortunate to have a PhD candidate from Antakya, Turkey at our College whom I have managed to get into contact with. His name is Berat Mahlioglku. Berat, who we now call "Berry" is not only a very intelligent gentleman but is extremely personable. We tried several titles using Turkish custom to address him, for example, Berat Bey, or more formally Mahliogiku hanimefendi. However, he's familiar with American English having studied at the American University of Beirut. We now address him as Professor Berry, with which he is quite delighted.

"However, after a lengthy discussion between the Rabbi and the Professor, I was informed by the Rabbi to advise you of a possible danger. The town of Antakya is built on the former Antioch of biblical fame. It once was a large and important city of the Roman Empire. In that city, the former Antioch, there are many denominations of both Christian and Muslim churches and mosques. To this day there is a church that is built on the location of a former one in the city, of Antioch, in which a document was discovered that we think predates the original canon gospels of the New Testament. In this document which is referred to as *The Lost Gospel* [3]there is a compilation of writing about Jesus Christ which predates the acceptance of Pauline Christianity by the Council of Nicaea in 325 AD. In that document, The Lost Gospel, it is stated in code, that Jesus was human and was married to Mary Madgalene and had children. I've prepared a list

---

[3]   Simcha Jacobovici, Barrie Wilson *The Lost Gospel, Decoding the Ancient Text that Reveals Jesus' Marriage to Mary the Magdalene, Translation of the Syriac Manuscript by Tony Burke,* New York, 2014

of references you can look up, but the book is about a document in the British Library known *as British Library manuscript #17,202.* I strongly suggest you obtain it and read it. When you do, and I strongly suggest that you do, you will understand why you must be extremely discreet. In the past people who have believed the contents and even practiced the faith based on it have been put to death as heretics. All modern Christian scholars will deny its validity. I believe we will plan for the codex which you have given us to be secretly conveyed to the Bishop in Antakya by courier, possibly Professor Berry."

"Is there any chance that someone who has this in their possession or claims that it is true would be put to death in this time of the Twenty First Century?" Elisheva asked.

"Probably not but the verbal condemnation could be grievous. In the Levant, Turkey, Syria, Iraq, who knows? Discretion is the better part of valor. Today, I will give you a paper copy and electronic copy of the translations of both the Sefer scroll and the codex. Both are annotated with references and footnotes. I'm sure that when your grandparents donate it to the Synagogue in the Bronx it will become a treasured scroll. It has been a real pleasure for me to have been chosen to conserve it. "Believe me, it has been a labor of love, both for the scroll and the codex. I have placed both documents and other material into this black canvas poly fabric bag that you can carry with its handles. It also has a detachable shoulder strap which greatly helps when boarding an airplane or walking through an airport pulling a suitcase behind you."

Jonah stood up and went to a cupboard and retrieved the black bag he has just described. He placed it on the desk.

"Pick it up," Elisheva, "and bring it to the next room. We will set it on the long table there, unpack it and go over all the contents one by one.

They spent the next two hours going over each item in the carrying case with Johah. Both Elisheva and Santiago were fascinated as he described each item and again emphasized how important and precious each document was to a large number of people who would come to know them.

They left the center with Johnah's wishes for a safe journey and to a rich future with the documents in hand. Elisheva carried it over her shoulder during the brief walk to the pickup and placed it on her lap after she entered the truck.

"Are you hungry?" She asked Santiago. "If so why don't we pick up something to eat then go back to the Airbnb?"

"We will." He replied. "My grandmother has a safe under the floor in the storage room. It's only used when a guest has some precious or valuable items he or she wants to place somewhere safe. Mostly it's for the purpose of people who come to Tucson for the Gem Show and want someplace safe to store their purchases. I change the combination after each user, but it's not used that much. It will be safe and secure there.

"How about after we eat, we put the bag in the safe and go to my parents to introduce you. I'm sure they would love to get to know you especially since I will be traveling to New York with you. I won't explain much after that, so they won't worry. Then we can stop by my apartment, and I can pack a suitcase and get my passport. It's still good for several more years. After that we can stop by my grandmother's so you can meet her."

"Great. I see hamburger drive through up ahead. I can go for a hamburger, fries and a coke."

"You've got it."

They returned to the Airbnb, unloaded the carrying case and food and sat down to enjoy their fast-food meal.

"This is a special and rare treat for me. I try to limit myself only occasionally to a burger and fries and almost never a cola." Elisheva said.

"I admit that I eat this type of meal more than just occasionally." Santiago replied. "I try to eat healthy most of the time and try to work out at the university gym, or Entertainment Center, as it's called these days. When I was stationed on the USS Wasp I made friends with a lot of the Marines in the expeditionary force. They were schooled in Krav Maga, which is a martial arts skill that Marines and Navy Special Ops sailors are trained in. They asked me to join them when they were in their individual training sessions. I learned quite a bit from them and became reasonably proficient in it. I made a lot of friends with the Marines. Santiago and Jaime were a little much for them so they called me Jim."

"I know! When I was in Israel I was introduced to Krav Maga by woman friend who was an instructor. When I decided to travel to Tucson, I took a refresher course at the synagogue gym. It's something I've never had to use but if I do I think I will be ready. What about you?"

"Speaking of eating, let me ask. Do you only eat kosher food?"

"Oy vey," she answered. "I am not that observant although I'm very careful when I'm with my grandparents. Even my mother doesn't observe kashrut when she's not with my grandparents. I could really get used to this Mexican food you have here in Tucson."

After they had eaten Santiago showed her where the safe was in the storage room. He unlocked the door and entered the room where there was a wooden floor built over the concrete foundation. He pressed down on one of the floorboards depressing it slightly. He reached into the opening and carefully pressed a lever. The cover to the space, approximately four feet by four feet, snapped open several inches energized by a depressed spring on two opposite sides. He lifted the cover and exposed a square safe door. On the door there was a shiny keyhole into which a key could be placed into the cylinder to unlock the safe. There was also a keypad with several numbers on it which could also be used to open the safe. He entered a combination of five letters and numbers to unlock the safe. When he opened the door Elisheva observed that the entire space was lined with a carpet.

"Place the carrying case gently into it." He advised.

After she had placed the case, handling it with the care of a precious possession, he locked the safe, replaced the cover and stood up.

"That's done. Let's drive to my parent's house and then to my apartment before we visit my abuela."

"You know, Jaime," she told him, "I trust you completely. You are the only one who can recover that now."

"No," he quickly answered. "I will write down the combination on a slip of paper. Disguise it like it's an address on Lee Street here in Tucson. Then put it where you think it will be safe in your purse, or even in your cell phone. That way you will always have access to it if anything should happen to me. Elisheva, I don't want there to be any secrets between us."

"Unless it's for your own safety."

"Do you think that time will come?"

"It's part of my Jewish upringing. The part of Eastern Europe we're planning to go may not be kindly disposed to what we are doing. I'm not sure how common the name Santiago might be there, so I'll refer to you as Jim, if it seems prudent to me. The way Jaimie is pronounced is very similar to Hymie. Hymie is a derogatory term for a Jew."

He didn't say anything for the next several minutes while they returned to the truck to drive to his parents' house.

"What are you thinking about?" She asked.

"I'm sorry. I learned in the service to visualize what could go wrong and what one should do if it occurred. I was just wondering. I've actually never been to Europe other than port visits with the ship and a few days visiting the local area."

"We'll be fine. You're correct, that's a good strategy for meeting unexpected situations. It's something I have done since I was a child, especially after hearing of my grandparent's escape from the Germans and how close they came to danger. Is that your parent's home?"

Santiago entered the circular driveway in front of a redbrick ranch style home. She could see a garage on one end and noticed the typically dry southwest desert landscaping. As they exited the truck and were walking to the door, she remarked on the flowers that were planted in front of the house.

"Did your mother plant these beautiful flowers?" She asked.

"Yes. My Dad helps out when she asks but he's kinda' like me. Gardening is not a pleasurable pastime for him as it is for my mother. He does like very much to do certain things. See that big barrel on the other side of the house? It's a rainwater capture system. Believe it or not it rains enough here in Tucson that he can capture water to keep Mom's flowers in good shape. He's also almost convinced Mom to convert the swimming pool into a huge water capture and containment system which would provide enough water for all her plants year-round. Since myself and my siblings have grown up and live on our own, they hardly use the pool anymore and my dad is not happy with the upkeep and expense of maintaining it when it's barely used. The one argument my mother has is her concern that the grandchildren won't have a place to swim when they visit."

"Do you have any children?" She asked as Santiago rang the doorbell.

"No. I have two nephews from my brother and two nieces and a nephew from my sister. My mother keeps hoping I'll deliver. She says she won't give up on me even though I'm over thirty."

Elisheva couldn't help but smile as Mrs. Valencia, an attractive woman answered the door.

"Jaime! It's good to see you. Please come in. And who is this pretty young lady with you?"

Enrigue kissed his mother on the cheek and replied: "Her name is Elisheva, but everyone calls her Ellie. She is staying at grandma's Airbnb. She is visiting Tucson to complete some research. After we leave here, we will visit her."

"My name is Connie." His mother said as she embraced Elisheva.

"It is a pleasure to meet you, Connie."

"Please, come into the living room and sit down. May I offer you something to drink? Water, a soft drink, tea?" Connie asked.

"We also have hot tea." Santiago interjected. "Mom and Dad like to have a cup of tea in the afternoon.

"I would love a cup of tea." Elisheva answered.

"Please, have a seat and I'll be right back. Jaime, go into your father's study and tell him to come out and meet Ellie."

Santiago soon returned followed by his father, Gene. A slightly graying man just slightly shorter in height than Santiago.

"Dad, this is Elisheva, Ellie for short. She's here in Tucson for a brief stay. She's staying at grandma's Airbnb. After we leave here, we'll stop by and visit grandma then back to my apartment to pack."

"Oh," his father questioned, you're taking a trip. Where to?"

"I'll be traveling to New York City with Ellie. She's doing some research with which I'm helping. There's a good chance we may travel to Europe as part of it."

Connie returned with a platter of cups for everyone accompanied by a large plate of Mexican wedding cookies. After everyone was served, they had a pleasant conversation. Elisheva spoke of her upbringing in New York but avoided many details. She did not want to reveal too much to his parents. She was concerned about how they might worry. She also believed the fewer of the actual details of their research others knew about, the better.

After an hour and a half of pleasant conversation they said goodbye and drove to Santiago's grandmother's home for another introduction and more tea. Angela was interested in what Elisheva thought of the Airbnb and what if anything she would like to see added or improved. Elisheva was extremely pleased at the location and the privacy the Airbnb offered and especially the nearby location to the University of Arizona. Once again, she was careful not to reveal the essentials facts of her research and intentions.

Santiago kissed his grandmother on the cheek as he bade her farewell. She wished them a safe and successful journey.

"Que les vaya bien." She said as they walked to the truck.

"Con el favor, Dios." He answered.

When they arrived at Santiago's apartment, he called to confirm Elisheva's reservation and was able to purchase a ticket on the same flight. She had a window seat and the closest to her he could reserve was an aisle seat on the same row and side. He then packed a suitcase and a carryon bag.

By the time he was through with all his preparations it was eight o'clock in the evening.

"Well is there anything you would like, Elisheva. A glass of wine, a cocktail or even a beer. I have some excellent Mexican and Dutch beer in the fridge."

"I would love a glass of merlot." She responded. "I'm impressed. You seem to have tastefully decorated your apartment."

"Most of what you see my mother and grandmother arranged, sometimes with the help of my sister."

After he had poured her a glass of wine and himself a Mexican beer, he sat down next to her.

"What now?" He asked. "Would you like me to drive you back to the Airbnb? Or would you like to spend the night here. I actually have two bedrooms in my apartment although usually the second I use as an office. But I do have a comfortable bed there."

"I'd love to stay here. I can sleep on the bed in your study. It's been a long day, and I am tired. I really would like to go to bed early. Maybe tomorrow we can get an early start to pack and drive to the airport. It's a "red eye" flight from Tucson direct to La Guardia. We will arrive in New York early in the morning and can get settled in my apartment."

CHAPTER SIX

———⸎⸎⸎⸎———

Big City Turn Me Loose and Set Me Free[4]

They arrived at La Guardia a little before five a.m. and were fortunate to catch a commuter bus directly to Grand Central Station. From there they took the subway to Elisheva's apartment in the Bronx. They were both tired from not having been able to catch much sleep on the red eye flight from Tucson.

"Welcome to my abode." She spoke. "I bet you are exhausted. I'm so tired all I want to do is place the carry bag in a safe place and go to sleep. What about you?"

"Sounds great."

She showed him how to pull down the wall bed which was made and ready. Her apartment resembled Santiago's Tucson apartment. Her second bedroom had been turned into a study and computer room complete with a wall bed. She reached up and pulled down the ready made wall bed.

Santiago washed his face and brushed his teeth. He stripped down to his shorts and pulled the bedcovers back and laid down. In seconds he was asleep.

He woke up and looked at the digital clock on the bedstand next to where he lay. It read 09:00 in bright red numbers. He could smell the aroma of coffee coming from somewhere. Probably she's in the kitchen he thought as he washed his face and brushed his teeth. He looked at the two-day stubble on his face and decided he would wait until later to shave.

"Good morning, sleepy head." Elisheva greeted.

---

[4]   Haggard, Merle, Holloway, Dean, from the Album Big City, 1982, Tract Two

"Good morning. I can't believe I slept nine hours. I guess it's jet lag. The coffee smells great."

"I recall you take just a smidgeon of cream and no sugar."

"Yes. Thanks."

She brought a cup of steaming hot coffee and sat it down next to him. I also have some bagels with cream cheese and lox. I'm not sure if you like lox but if not, I have peanut butter and jelly. What's your preference, Sir?"

"Boy, the peanut butter and jelly sounds awful tempting but, when in New York, do as the New Yorkers do. I'll try the cream cheese and lox."

"You've never had bagels, lox and cream cheese before!" She exclaimed in mock surprise with her eyes wide open.

"I'll bet you've never tried menudo either," he replied as he savored the gulp of coffee.

"I promise I'll try it the next time we have an opportunity." She said as she sat across the small circular table from him.

"This is a really nice apartment you have, Ellie. I'm not really knowledgeable about New York apartments but this has got to cost you a pretty penny."

"Actually, we're right next to my grandparent's home. Remember the steps we took from the street to the door last night?"

"Yes. It felt like the last leg of a marathon."

"The stairs to the left of the ones we took lead up to my grandparent's house. My mother also lives with them. After the war, when my grandparents settled here in the Bronx, prices were not what they are now. When my mother was planning to get married, her parents, my grandparents, purchased this one and had it renovated for the newlyweds. That way, they would have their daughter and any grandchildren right next to them. It may not seem intuitively obvious to you but when most of your family was murdered by the Germans you have a predilection for being close to what family remains. After my father passed, they remodeled it so that I could have this nice apartment and another renter could also live here. That way the rent could pay for my utilities."

"I really admire your grandparents. I'm sure you've inherited your brains from them as well as your mom. What was your father's name again?"

"Morris Gurwitz. Gurwitz is the Polish spelling. The Russian spelling is Gurevich, but there are also many variations. One of the things my mother told me about my father is that he was into genealogy. Apparently, his family were originally Sephardic Jews who were expelled from Spain during the Edict of Expulsion in 1492. That's similar to what your family experienced. They also settled in Bohemia, in a town called Horodice, then later in Prague where there was a large Jewish community established there. From Prague they were kicked out by Princess Theresa and went into Russia. That was about as far as he got into his family's past. My mother saved his notes and one day would like to look further into his genealogy. One of the things the two of us discovered from reading a Jewish newsletter about genealogy, is that the Horowitz lineage can be traced back to the Second Temple, about 586 BCE or so. Like you said, Sepharad is the Hebrew name for Hispania, the Roman name for the Iberian Peninsula."

"I am very impressed, Elisheva. The more I get to know you the more I am impressed. You fit my definition of an overachiever. Let me ask you a question. Back in Tucson you asked me if I was a devout Catholic. I told you that I was not as pious nor as observant as my parents and grandmother. I also told you about my attempt to learn more about my genealogy when I learned that my grandmother came from a family of converso Jews. What about you? I'm pretty sure that your grandparents are devout."

She didn't answer for a brief minute. *I am beginning to believe this man in front of me may finally be my soul mate, the one I will maybe want to spend the rest of my life with and perhaps, have his children.*

"Bear with me, Jaime. I believe in the Creator. I believe that he created not only this world, but the universe. One of the titles of the creator in Jewish prayer is *King of the Universe.* One of the questions many before me have asked is why is there evil in this world? If God is all powerful, omnipotent, then why can't he prevent evil in the world? If he is omnipotent, and allows evil to occur in the world, does that mean he is not all good, or omnibenevolent?

"There has been much evil in mankind's history, even prehistory. For example, the Holocaust perpetuated on the Jews by the Germans is so egregiously evil that it caused a *disturbance in the Force,* to quote from Star Wars.

"The treatment of the Jews by Spain during the Inquisition when they were tortured and burned at the stake is another supremely egregious crime against humanity that also caused the so-called disturbance of the Force.

"There are many more examples, but just those are enough to give me pause as to what is the reason for so much suffering. I know what the clerics say, the rabbis and the ministers and the priests and others: they say God has a plan for all of us, for each and every one of us. We, with our finite minds and spirit can't possibly comprehend what the infinite mind of God has in mind for us. Therefore, we must have faith and trust in the Creator.

"I don't accept this. I don't know about you but there has to be a better explanation for the thread of evil that has been woven into the fabric of our human history. Remember when Jonah Weisenberg told us about a book that had been written called the Lost Document?"

"Yes I do. He told us that in that book it discusses documents which preceded Pauline Christianity. If I remember correctly, he admonished us to read it. He also told us that in that book there is a dicussion of a codex at least as old as the New Testament Gospels, if not older, which discusses Jesus being married to Mary Magdalene and having children."

"You're correct. It seems that these documents which were at least as old as or older than the New Testament, had to be hidden because they were declared heretical by the Roman Emperor's Christian supporters. That made it necessary to hide in plain sight, or to code it so that the contents would not be obvious. To fail to do that one could be charged with heresy and banned into exile, or worse yet, burned at the stake!

"I'm going to go down to Abe's bookstore about two blocks from here. He is a vendor for several national bookstores and vendors. I'll pick up two copies of The Lost Gospel, one for each of us. I am anxious to learn about the codex which was at least as old as the New Testament in which Jesus was described as human and married to Mary Magdalene and had children."

"I'll go with you. When are you going to tell your mother that we are here."

"I called her this morning and told her we would drop by to see them and to introduce you to the family this evening. I told her we wanted to rest and plan our next few days here. When she said that she understood she sounded to me that she had some kind of motherly perception of what I told her."

"I don't know. Are we still going to Prague in the near future?"

"Maybe, maybe not. Very frequently the synagogue sponsors guided tours to the Holy Land. It would be easy for us to be part of the tour to get into Israel and then break off and travel on our own. I spent two months of my summer vacation in Israel when I was a junior in High School. It was easy to make friends and travel mostly unsupervised by our counselors, who often were not much older than we were and wanted to explore like us. Let's wait until after we read the Lost Gospel as Jonah Weisenberg recommended."

It was a pleasant walk to the bookstore. Although Santiago had been to big cities before when in the service, he was still impressed by the amount of people of all descriptions that were crowding the sidewalks and street corners. He took the curbside and was pleased when Elisheva placed her arm in his. At Abe's Book Store, Elisheva went to the Will Call desk to pick two copies of The Lost Gospel. On the return trip they stopped at a corner store and bought two ice cream cones. Once back at the apartment Elisheva boiled hot water and served each a cup of tea and a sweet biscuit. They sat across the table from each other and soon became involved in reading.

"Listen to this." Elisheva told him. *"Decoding the Ancient Text that Reveals Jesus' Marriage to Mary the Magdalene.* Let's read for at least the next hour, take notes, and then compare what we've read."

"OK." He replied. "I'm going into the living room where I can be comfortable with my notebook."

In only a few minutes Santiago asked: "Ellie, what does it mean on the dedication page where Simcha Jacobovici writes: *Dedicated to Ammon Rosenfeld (z'l) scholar, friend and truth seeker (1944-2014).*"

"It is Hebrew and literally means "memories for blessing". It is usually translated as "may his memory be a blessing". Zichrono brachen for a man and zichrona brachen for a woman."

"I remember you told me that you attended Hebrew school as well as the public schools. Do you speak Hebrew?"

"Well enough to get by in Israel during my summer study there. It comes back pretty quick when you're immersed in it."

"You speak English, Yiddish and Hebrew. Wow!"

"You speak English and Spanish. I also remember that you took two years of German in college. Do you speak that well enough to get by in the German speaking countries?"

"I can read some well enough to usually get a basic understanding of it. It is the spoken German and its variations in some areas and countries that I can have difficulty with. I don't think I would starve or die of thirst. I can get along well enough using the translate function on my cell phone if I have to.

"Hopefully, I won't disturb you during the next hour, but I just had to know what the characters of the blessing meant."

They read intensively for the next two hours, finally pausing to take a break and stretch.

"So, Jaime, ready to compare notes? What have you've written down so far?"

"I am pretty much captivated by what I've read. OK:

"One: Right at the beginning it states that they will decode the text to show that there is evidence that Jesus was married to Mary Magdalene and had children together.

"Two: The authors also insert the caveat that no one should get their knickers in a twist. They are not discussing theology, just stating what they've read in a document that has been sitting in a library for a long time.

"Three: They discuss another document that was also known to some few scholars out of the mainstream called the Didache. They write that it gives a glimpse into pre-Pauline Christianity and that the sharing of bread and wine was simply a thanksgiving meal in memory of the Last Supper and was not meant to be thought of as the actual body and blood of Christ, as it is blieved today in Catholic doctrine.

"Four: They also refer to another mysterious text titled Joseph and Aseneth. Before I could really understand what they were referring to I had to review the Old Testament story about Jacob's favorite son, Joseph.

"I've reread the text of Genesis reviewing all about Joseph, how his brothers sold him into slavery and how he endured some tribulations until he was called by Pharoah to interpret his dreams. You may remember that he interpreted Pharoah's dreams to mean Egypt would experience seven years of plenty then seven years of famine. This came true and Pharoah made him second only to himself."

"Yes! I am familiar with that part of Genesis and Jacob, whom God later named Israel."

"To reward Joseph, *Pharoah gave him the name Zapenath-panes and gave him Asenath daughter of Potiphar, priest of On, as his wife.[5]*"

"Asenath is again mentioned only once more: *Before the years of famine came, Joseph had two sons whom Asenath daughter of Potiphar, priest of On, bore to him. Joseph gave the firstborn Manessa, for he said God has made me forget all my hardship and all my father's house. The second he named Ephraim, for God has made me fruitfaul in the land of my misfortunes.[6]*

"The authors of the Lost Gospel refer to *typology,* which they describe as a process by which the new Christian movement created a history for itself by usurping the Hebrew Bible for Christian purposes.[7]

"They say that the text of Joseph and Aseneth is a coded document that represents Joseph as a stand in for Jesus and Aseneth as a stand in for Mary Magdalene and give reasons why. They describe this later work as a coded document, coded, because of the existential threat of going against the prevailing Pauline Christianity of the Roman Empire. It is coded to prevent being declared heresy or worse, exile and possibly being burned at the stake.

"This was true during the very early history of Christianity. There were several sects which regarded Jesus as an ordinary man. The Ebionites were one such sect.

"*The Ebionites embraced an adoptionist Christology, thus understanding Jesus of Nazareth as a mere man who, by virtue of his righteousness in following the Law of Moses, was chosen by God to be the messianic prophet like Moses. A majority of the Ebionites rejected as heresies the orthodox Christian beliefs in Jesus' divinity, virgin birth and substitutionary atonement that were accepted by the early Church; and therefore maintained that Jesus was born the natural son of Joseph and Mary, sought to abolish animal sacrifices by prophetic proclamation, and died as a martyr in order to move all Israel to repentance.[8]*

---

5   Gen 41:45

6   Gen 41: 50-52

7   Simcha Jacobovici, Barrie Wilson *The Lost Gospel, Decoding the Ancient Text that Reveals Jesus' Marriage to Mary the Magdalene, Translation of the Syriac Manuscript by Tony Burke,* New York, 2014, p54

8   https://en.wikipedia.org/wiki/Ebionites

"The bottom line, Ellie, is, I believe that the coded text referred to is a Christian document and not a Jewish one. The reason it is coded is to preclude suffering the consequences of being declared heritical with unsavory consequences such as being burned at the stake, exile or banishment."

"Wow! Now it's my turn to be impressed. I pretty much agree with most of what you wrote down. Not simply as a side note but two things I think you should know about which originate from Freud, Jung, and Immanual Velikovsky."

She left her chair and went into the study to retrieve a well-worn notebook with many colorful tabs that obviously marked references she wanted to quickly refer to. She returned and sat down on the chair, opened the notebook and began to speak.

"Jaime, have you ever heard of Carl Gustav Jung?"

"Yes. I took Psychology 101 in college, and I remember reading about him."

"Do you know what he defined as an archetype?"

"Kind of. Something ancient or archaic that all humans are aware of?"

"Close enough. Let me read you, his definition; *Archetype – a universal symbol or pattern that are present in the collective unconscious of all humans.*[9] To my knowledge Jung never said what caused the archetypes but he found them through his work as a clinical psychiatrist.

"Number two. Have you ever heard of Immanuel Velikovsky?[10]"

"Yes! I have. I know his works pretty well. He wrote a book titled *Worlds in Collision*[2] among other works. In his works he wrote what is essentially a forensic study of ancient texts, myths, legends and traditions from all over the world indicating the heaven we see today above us was drastically different from thousands of years ago. Very briefly, he was labeled as a crackpot by some prominent astronomers because they said what he described could not have possibly happened under the law of gravity discovered by Isaac Newton. They were correct."

---

[9]   Carl Gustav Jung, The Portable Jung, Edited by Joseph Campbell, New York, Penguin Books,1976,52

[10]   Immanuel Velikovsky, Worlds in Collision (Garden City, New York: Doubleday & Company, Inc, 1950)

"Exactly! Newton only discussed gravity, much like Albert Einstein. But gravity is billions of times weaker than the electromagnetic force and may even be caused by asymmetrical alignment of subatomic particles. Now, we both can agree that this Russian Jew had some insightful understanding. Listen, I am going to read you a verse from the Tanach, the first five books of the Jewish Bible, or the Old Testament, in Christian terms."

She placed her tattered notebook on the table and picked up her copy of the bible, also with several colorful tabs on the edges of pages to mark a reference. She turned to a green tab and opened the book and began to read.

"This is from the book of Isaiah, Chapter 34:[11]

"Come near, you nations, and listen:
    Pay attention, you peoples!
Let the earth hear, and all that is in it,
    the world, and all that comes out of it!
The Lord is angry with all nations;
    his wrath is on all their armies.
He will totally destroy them,
    He will give them over to slaughter.
Their slain will be thrown out,
    Their dead bodies will stink;
The mountains will be soaked with their blood.
All the stars in the sky will be dissolved
    And the
heavens rolled up like a scroll;
All the starry host will fall
    Like withered leaves from the vine;
    Like shriveled figs from the fig tree."

"That, Jaime, is a quote from the Tanach that makes theologians say that the God of the Old Testament was a God of wrath and anger, a God of vengeance. Isaiah was prophesizing about the subjugation of Judah by Assyria. Consider those words for a few minutes."

After a few minutes she picked up the bible again and chose an orange tab from which she opened another page.

---

[11]   Isa 14

"One more quick quote from Isaiah. Like all prophets in the Old Testament many believed that they received a divine mission from the Creator. Here, Isaiah is prophesizing about the destruction of the Babylonian empire, the death of Sennacherib and that of Nebuchadnezzar:

"For the stars of heaven and the constellations thereof shall not give their light.[12] Therefore I will shake the heavens and the earth shall remove out of her place, in the wrath of the Lord of hosts, and in the day of his fierce anger.[13]"

"One thing we can both agree on, Elle, is that what Immanuel Velikovsky was writing about in Worlds in Collision was a really complex subject. Suffice it to say that at one time earth was part of a binary star system called a brown dwarf star which included Saturn, Jupiter, Venus, Mars, and Earth in a locked phase array. A brown dwarf star system is conducive to evolution because it is contained within a sheaf which permits photosynthesis and the development of life. This brown dwarf star was traveling through space until it eventually entered our present solar system and was captured by the electromagnetic attraction of our greater star we know as the sun. As the brown dwarf star was captured and integrated into our solar system there were changes that affected not only the brown dwarf star, but our original solar system as well. Initially some of the effects were benign and were held in awe by our human ancestors that had evolved in what at that time had been an extremely conducive environment for life and evolution, a Garden of Eden, so to speak. But other changes caused the orbits of the planets, specifically Saturn, Jupiter, Venus, Mars, and Earth to change as well as Mercury, which may have been one of the original planets of our solar system before the dwarf star entered. These changes, perturbations, caused the orbits of the planets to change and were witnessed by humans living here at the time. Some of these changes in orbit caused catastrophic and terrifying events which made some people fear the end of the world was happening. That, is probably the origin of the archetype of the end of the world, or eschatology."

"I totally agree with that. We now can estimate that there are probably millions of such brown dwarf brown stars. I think we both agree that science, myth, and religion can be all related. There was

---

[12] Isa 13:10

[13] Isa 13:13

a time when Velikovsky's ideas were dismissed but that has changed with the emergence of plasma physics and the Electric Universe[14]. Let me cite just one more example of how religion can interpret eschatological fears.

"Moses ben Maimon, also known as Maimonides, or RamBam was a Sephardic Jew who became one of the most influential and prolific writers in the Middle Ages. He is still studied and quoted to this day, believe it or not, and still has quite a bit of influence on Jewish thought and commentary. But, to illustrate how people cannot accept the fact that such catastrophic events actually occurred let me quote to you what he said when writing comments about the quotes from Isaiah."

Once again she picked up her tattered notebook and turned to a page with a purple tab.

"When referring to Isaiah, Maimonides writes: *Will any person who has eyes to see find in these verses any expression that is obscure, or that might lead him to think that they contain an account of what will befall the heavens? The prophet means to say that the individuals, who were like stars as regards their permanent, high and undisturbed position, will quickly come down? He essentially states that the prophet is speaking in metaphors because, to his experience, the world has essentially remained the way it was since creation.* Remember, this was long before archeologists found perpendicular whales in the Himalayas.

"The point I am making, Jaime, is that historical events are open to interpretation and in many instances religious leaders seek to make the past conform to what they believe is the divine plan of creation. But they can be mistaken, and often are. One good example is our discussion about the divinity of Jesus before Pauline Christianity assumed the mantle of the official Roman Empire religion by Constantine. He did this, history records, in order to unite his empire into one, sanctioned Christianity."

"Jaime," she said, "you should let your beard grow out for a few more days. It is very attractive. Why don't we take a break now, relax and get ready to meet my mother and grandparents for dinner tonight.

---

[14]   Wallace Thornhill and David Talbott, The Electric Universe (Portland, 2007)

CHAPTER SEVEN

———∿∽◦∾◦⟲⊷◯⊷⟳◦∾◦∿———

brukhim hbim tsu meyn heym aun mshpkh
(Welcome to my home and family)
Yiddish welcome

Elisheva would have normally pressed the doorbell and walked in. She knew the door would be unlocked if her grandparents and mother knew she was coming for a visit. She paused until the door was opened by her grandmother.

"Shalom aleikhem!" Dinah greeted. "Elisheva, it is so good to see you! You look well."

"Aleikhem shalom!" Elisheva responded hugging her grandmother and kissing her on the cheek.

"Grandmother, this is Santiago Valencia, or Jaime as everyone calls him."

"Actually, I prefer you to call me Jim." He said remembering the derogatory Hymie.

Dinah released her grand daughter and took Santiago's hand. Welcome, Jim, please come in. It is truly a pleasure to meet you."

"Shalom Aleikhem." Santiago greeted as she pulled him towards her. She embraced him with a warm, welcoming hug.

"Aleikhem shalom." Dinah replied. "Are you Jewish?"

"Not yet grandma, he's in training!" Elisheva joyfully retorted with a laugh.

Dinah holding Santiago's hand, led the two of them into the living room where Elisheva's mother and grandfather were sitting. Both arose.

"Hello, mother." Elisheva said as she hugged Esther and kissed her on the cheek.

"Grandpa!" She exclaimed as she hugged Schlomo and gave him a kiss on the cheek."

After exchanging greetings with everyone Schlomo sat down in his recliner and spoke: "Please, Jim, have a seat. We are anxious to meet any young man that is a friend of Elisheva."

"Ellie, give bubbe and me a hand in the kitchen." Esther told her daughter.

"I'll be right back, Jim. Don't go away!" She teased.

"I'm not going anywhere! I like it here!" He retorted.

Schlomo laughed.

"So," he asked Santiago, "what do you think of New York so far. Have you ever been here before?"

"No, sir." He replied. "I have been to some big cities before but not like this one. It makes me wonder how anyone ever finds their way around."

"It's not difficult once you learn the ropes. I believe I heard one of the women say that Ellie told them you were in the Navy. What did you do?"

"I was an Intelligence Specialist which essentially meant I was trained in information warfare. I was on a large ship that carried a Marine Expeditionary Force with it and included landing craft, helicopters and fighter aircraft including some of the most modern, the F35."

"I'm impressed. Did you graduate from college?"

"Yes, I have a degree in Electrical Engineering."

"Tell me, Jim, were there any Jewish sailors or marines aboard your ship?"

"Yes, there were. We had a Chaplain aboard our ship, and he would give services not only aboard our ship, which is pretty big, but also the supporting ships, like destroyers and frigates. He would be helo'd from our ship to the others. Sometimes, when there were enough Jewish sailors on the other ships he would be accompanied by a Jewish Lay Leader and would be transported to other ships with the Chaplain. I understand that if there were a Jewish Lay Leader aboard they would hold services on Friday. But when she went aboard with the Chaplain she would hold Torah study. She was what the Navy calls and Operations Specialist, so I worked with her in my duty station. The Navy calls it the Combat Information Center or CIC."

"It sounds as if you're giving my husband a lesson about the Navy. I heard what you told him about the girl who was a Jewish Lay Leader. Did you know which congregations she was with?" Dinah asked.

"Reconstructionist but I'm not sure what that is." Santiago replied.

"Oy, ve iz mir!" Schlomo exclaimed.

"Oy gevalt!" Dina exclaimed. "That is not even Jewish."

"Don't worry about it, Grandpa, "Elisheva said as she brought a tray of snacks, setting it on the table across from where Schlomo sat.

After they had shared the snacks, they had a discussion of Tucson and Santiago's parents and grandmother. It so happened that today, October 28, was a Friday.

"You're in luck, Jim," Elisheva said. "This evening is the beginning of Shabbat. You will be able to share this with us"

"I'm looking forward to it. I have read about it in my studies about crypto Jews, but I haven't actually participated in a Shabbat meal." He asked.

"Don't worry. I will explain everything to you as we go along."

"Tell him, Ellie, that we just observed Simchat Torah and now we are starting a new year of reading the bible again." Schlomo told her.

"I will, Grandpa, but we don't want to give him so much information that he will be inundated and become exasperated."

Schlomo only smiled at her.

"OK, take it easy. Just a brief description."

"Jim, Simchat Torah simply means Rejoicing of the Torah. It's a joyous religious observance held on the last day of Sukkot, or the Festival of Booths."

"I've actually heard of that in my catechism class. The Festival of Booths is mentioned in the New Testament, I believe. It's where Jews build outdoor booths or living quarters to remember their wandering in the desert." Santiago added. "I am also aware of it in my studies."

"We actually built a booth on the balcony on one of our second story rooms!" Schlomo said with a twinkle in his eye.

"Yes, we did." Ellisha confirmed. "It wasn't a very elaborate one like some build who have a back yard. When I was a child one of my friend's fathers actually built one in her tree house in which the entire family spent one night. Ours was just an ad hoc arrangement of a tarp and some yarn to secure it to the balcony railing. Unfortunately, it rained one night and all of us got wet. But it was fun and something we shared as a family.

"Not to belabor the point, Jim, it usually occurred during the harvest when the wandering Israelites would gather the fruits and grains and take them into their makeshift huts. Simchat Torah then begins on the last day of Sukkot, which is the name of the Festival of Booths. That is when the last portion of the Torah is read, and we begin again with the next cycle of reading. All the Torah scrolls are carried from their Ark and paraded around the synagogue seven times in a joyous procession. Grandpa was carrying one of the scrolls. Everyone is singing and dancing followed by the children waving flags. There are also many sweets given out and eaten."

Both Schlomo and Elisheva looked at Santiago to see how he reacted to her explanation.

"I see." Santiago told them. "It is somewhat similar to what the Catholics do with their reading of the New Testament. I understand it's also celebrated but I've never witnessed anything like you described. I'm impressed."

He looked at Schlomo who happily smiled at him.

"Good." The older man told him, obviously pleased at his granddaughter's explanation.

"Ellie," Dinah said as she entered the room, "my calendar says sunset tonight in at five fifty-eight p.m."

"Let me check." Elisheva replied.

She took out her cell phone and selected the App which would tell her the precise time of sunset in New York and when to light the Sabbath candles.

"The time to light the candles is five forty p.m., Grandma."

"Exactly." Dinah responded. "Come, lets go into the dining room."

When they entered the dining room Esther was standing next to the table resplendent with a beautiful tablecloth and dinner settings for six.

After several minutes of conversation, Dinah took a box of wooden matches and as the clock on the wall indicated five forty p.m., she struck the match and lit the candles.

"Cover your eyes, Jaime." Elisheva told him. He did so then heard Dinah pray.

"Baruch atah Adonai, Eloheinu Melech haolam, asher kid'shanu b'mitzvotav v'tzivanu l'hadlik ner shel Shabbat. (Blessed are you, Adonai our God, ruler of the universe, who has sanctified us through your mitzvot and commanded us to kindle the Shabbat candles)".

"Uncover your eyes, Jaime." She told him.

He did as she said and saw that the two candles were lit.

Schlomo, then spoke.

"My children will serve God all the days of their lives and honor His Word and be blessed all the days of their lives. No harm will touch my children. Only blessings will come upon my children. Blessings are being sent to my children each and every day by the love of God."

"That blessing is from Psalm 35:27." Elisheva said. "Now Grandpa will recite the Kiddush or blessing of the wine."

Schlomo stood at the head of the table and spoke.

"And there was evening and there was morning, the sixth day.

The heaven and the earth were finished, and all their array. On the seventh day God finished the work that God had been doing, and God ceased on the seventh day from all the work that God had done. And God blessed the seventh day and declared it holy, because on it God ceased from all the work of creation that God had done."

"Come on, Jim" Elisheva said. "Let's wash our hands before we eat."

When all had washed their hands and returned to the dining room, Dinah removed a cloth which covered a loaf of bread that had a twist to it.

Esther then told Santiago: "This is the challah, or Sabbath bread. It reminds us of the cycle of life, of the harvested bread we need to keep ourselves alive. It also reminds us to make our lives worthwhile."

Esther then prayed: "Blessed are you, Adonai our God, ruler of the universe, who brings forth bread out of the earth."

"Elisheva told Santiago: "Jim, take your cup of wine, and we'll drink."

He did as she instructed, as did the others. Schlomo then said: "L'chaim."

"L'chaim!" The others answered.

Esther took the loaf of bread and tore it into several pieces. She salted her piece then passed the saltshaker to Elisheva, who salted the piece of bread she had taken.

"Why do we salt the bread?" Santiago asked, accepting the saltshaker and salting his bread before passing it to Dinah.

"We do it in remembrance of the sacrifices given at the Temple in Jerusalem, which were all salted before making an offering to the altar. Also, it is written in Genesis: "By the sweat of your brow, you get bread to eat." Schlomo said as he salted his piece of bread.

"Now, everyone, please be seated."

Dinner was a pleasant affair discussing not only the day's events but asking Santiago about his time in the Navy.

It was nine thirty p.m. when they bade farewell to her family and Santiago and Elisheva returned to her apartment.

After they were comfortable in the living room Elisheva asked: "Well, Jaime, what do you think of my family and of Shabbat?"

"I have a very good feeling, Ellie. I feel serene and tranquil. It's almost as if a door to a deeper understanding is opening for me. Reading about my family's history is one thing, but actually experiencing some of the rituals is different."

"In what way?"

"Earlier, I remember you saying something to the effect that one shouldn't suffer for being Jewish. But this evening with your family was meaningful to me in a way that I can feel but can't quite yet explain."

"Well, we'll have plenty of time together to see how your feeling develops."

She walked over to where he was sitting on the sofa and straddled his lap and placed her arms around him. She kissed him tenderly, then holding his face in her hands, she kissed him with a lingering passionate kiss, rubbing his lips with her tongue. She could feel him pressing against her.

"Come." She said and led him by the hand into her bedroom.

Once in the bedroom he slowly unbuttoned his shirt. He removed it and dropped it to the floor. He unbuckled his belt and unbuttoned his trousers tugging them and his shorts down to the floor. He stepped out of them and his shoes. She looked him in the eyes as she pulled her blouse off and let it fall onto the carpet. She then pulled her pants and panties down around her feet, still looking him in the eyes but she could see him throbbing in her peripheral vision. He placed his arms around her and gently laid her on he back. She pulled him gently on top of her. She had her first climax with his finger, her second with his tongue and the last one together with him exploding into a shared ecstasy. The lay together naked, holding each other and gently stroking each other's face and hair and tenderly sharing kisses.

"I love you." She told him.

"I love you." He replied.

There were no further words until the light of dawn softly entered into the bedroom. It gently bathed them with a light that seemed to cover them with an awakening of a new love in their lives.

He awoke and turning to his side to face her saw that she had already been on her side, looking at him while he slept and awakened.

CHAPTER EIGHT

—⁓⌖⌖⁓—

The point is love. Love, for it is love that you
are. Love, for it is love that all is.
American Proverb.

"Welcome to my world." She told him with a smile. "Are you sure you want to enter it?"

He looked at her and answered her with his smile. The look in his eyes answered as he spoke.

"Yes!"

Before he could say anything else she took his hand and led him out of bed.

"I like the way you look and the way I feel but we should put our pajamas on just in case someone knocks on our door. I'm going to wash my face and brush my teeth. I'll meet you in the kitchen and we can plan our day."

When he entered the kitchen, she was busy at the counter.

"Have a seat." She told him. "I've already poured your coffee and the cream is right next to you. I will soon have our bagels toasted and the cream cheese and lox are already on the table."

"I'm beginning to like bagels, cream cheese and lox. Especially the way you serve it. I'm hungry this morning."

"I can understand why, Mr. Valencia. We both consumed a lot of calories last night."

She brought the plate with the bagels and kissed him before placing them on the table and sitting down.

"What's on your mind, this morning?" She asked taking a bite of her bagel and a sip of coffee.

"I slept like a baby last night. But this morning when I woke up, I realized that I had a lot of things running through my mind."

"Tell me."

"Ok. I'll just throw them out and won't discuss them at any length just to let you know. What about David Finklestein? I realize I was deeply moved by what I experienced with you and your family last night. Your comments about the way Jews have been treated and what the clerics say does not make it right. Also, the Lost Gospel and the document continue to intrigue me even more. And I know that I want to be a part of your life and you to share mine. There!"

"Wow! I'm glad I asked! I know you love me, and I know beyond any possible doubt that I love you and want to share my life with you. Speaking of sharing, I believe we are about to share a deeply intriguing adventure that will bring meaning to us.

"Look. I've also been thinking. I'm going to call David and take the train to see him in Manhattan. We'll have lunch together and I'll tell him about you and that I've started a new chapter in my life. If we're not able to get together for lunch, I'll wait until he's off work or can take off. I don't want to rush our breakup. I owe that much to him. He's a good man and he has always treated me with respect. My family also is very fond of him, but they will understand.

"While I'm gone, why don't you take the opportunity to go over what we've talked about before. Did you know that we can enter Israel as Americans without having to get an Israeli visa. Israelis with an Israeli passport can enter Turkey for 90 days without a visa. I'm not sure about Americans but you can look it up while I'm gone."

"I'll do that." He answered.

"Good. You know where everything is. Don't worry about supper. I'll pick something up on the way home. I call you when I'm enroute."

It was nine a.m. when she kissed him goodbye.

"Be safe." He said as she turned to walk away. "Se vaya bien. Vaya con Dios."

She turned, smiling, and with a thrown kiss from her lips was gone.

He slowly closed the door. He went to her study and began to search requirements for entering Israel and Turkey. He was surprised to learn how easy it was to enter both countries. He found the website to apply for an *evisa*, or electronic visa. The website informed him he could complete it by answering several questions and paying online. The entire process could take as little as three minutes to complete.

He then returned to the kitchen to pour himself another cup of coffee and sat down. He once again to read the book, The Lost Gospel, and everything both he and Elisheva had discussed and taken notes about.

After two hours of reading and making notes, he was more convinced than ever that there was more to what he had learned about Christianity when he was taking catechism classes as a youth. He sat back in the recliner and let his mind quietly scroll through what he had been reading. Suddenly, he remembered that Jonah Weisenberg had mentioned that they thought the Turkish professor, Professor Berry as he recalled, would probably be selected to deliver the conserved codex to the Bishop of Antioch. He was from Antakya. I wonder when he will make the delivery. I'll ask Ellie to call and see if maybe he can meet us there so we can actually visit the site where the lost document was discovered.

He was renewed now with a purpose, to determine how they could get to Istanbul and then Antakya. He was able to determine that there were connecting flights between Istanbul and Antakya with a distance of 511 miles. He also learned that they could fly direct from Istanbul to Prague by several airlines including the Turkish national airline. An American entering the Czech Republic did not need a visa for a stay of less than ninety days. Flights were also available from Prague direct to JFK Airport in New York City for a reasonable price. When Elisheva returned they could work out an itinerary and the cost of air travel.

It was a little after seven in the evening when Elisheva returned carrying a brown paper bag. He met her at the door and kissed her.

"Here, let me help with your stuff. What's in the large brown paper bag.?"

"Two Reuben sandwiches on Jewish rye with a kosher dill pickle and some freshly made Cole slaw. I thought we could have this for supper with a cup of hot tea."

"It sounds good to me."

After they had completed eating and sharing pleasant conversation about how her trip to Manhattan went, they cleared the table and washed dishes. After everything was put away, she looked at him.

"Okay. Let's sit down and I'll tell you how it went with David. Then you can tell me what you did today."

"Agreed." He answered.

He sat down on the recliner across the table from her.

"To be honest with you, Elisheva, I would like to know how it went with you and David. But, if you don't want to go into certain details, that's quite all right with me."

"It went kinda' like I thought it would, but it turned out to have been better than I hoped for. I was able to meet David for a late lunch. He was tied up at noon with an important customer that needed assistance in obtaining some documents for his tax accountant. David was able to assist him. I waited for him across the street at a downtown bar and grill that catered to the clientele surrounding the banks and other offices in that area.

"I could tell immediately when I saw him enter that he wore an expression of concern that I have come to know when he is upset or is expecting bad news. Who says only women have intuition? I was nursing one of those popular coolers with about five percent alcohol and with a tasty lime flavor. He sat down and ordered Selzer. He was expecting to return to work and alcohol on one's breath is strictly a *no-no*.

"I reached out across the table and took his hands into mine. David, I began, but he soon interrupted me.

"Ellie, he began, we've known each other for a long time, and we have become very close. So close that I was going to ask you to marry me. I know in my heart that you are going to break up with me. Am I right?"

"David, I was hoping that we could discuss our futures. Yes, I was not ready to make a lifetime commitment when I last saw you before leaving for Tucson, but I honestly expected that you would propose to me, and I would accept. You know my grandparents, Schlomo and Dinah Rosenberg fled Germany just before it would have been too late. They brought with them two very old and sacred documents. You didn't know about this because my Grandfather was waiting for the right time to have it restored, the term is conserved, but swore us to secrecy to never tell anyone about it until he decided when the time was right. When I learned about it I was moved. When a Rabbi came to visit, my grandfather brought it out and showed both documents to him, I was again very deeply moved. One was a Sefer scroll from the synagogue in his shtetl from which he and my grandmother fled and the other was an ancient Christian codex with a secretive and troubled past. Both of these documents deeply affected me and made me realize that I deeply wanted to become more involved with them.

"To make a long story short, my grandfather and a very holy Rabbi found a conservator of Sefer scrolls at the University of Arizona in Tucson. They planned to courier it to the conservator. I was to follow up and receive an electronic and annotated printed copy of both. While there I met a man, about our age, with whom I have come to develop a deep relationship with."

"Do you love him?"

"Yes."

"Is he Jewish."

"No, or at least not yet."

"You know it is a Shanda to marry a goy."

"You were always like me, David. We are not as observant as our parents and grandparents. Through out Jewish history there have always been interfaith marriages. Look at Moses."

"Yes, but it was always understood that when we married we would bring our children up Jewish, and you would keep kashrut. Now you are giving all that up?"

"No. Jaime, that is his nickname. Jaime is short for Santiago. Jaime and I are not only involved in a romantic relationship but in a spiritual journey together. I have always told you about how I feel that Jews have always been able to persevere and keep their faith through persecutions, pogroms and massacres throughout our history because of a strong spiritual belief in our faith. I was hoping that you would understand."

"You're swapping me for a Mexican?"

"I was stunned when he said that. He must have seen the look on my face because after several seconds of silence, during which neither one of us said a word, he apologized."

"Ellie, I'm sorry. I'm truly sorry for what I just said. Believe me, I did not mean it. I know in my heart that you are truly in love. I can see a certain look in your eyes and demeanor about you that I never saw when you were with me, even during those times when we made love together. I now realize that it is finally over between you and me and I accept it, not without some pain, but I accept it and if he makes you happy then I am glad for you."

"Thank you, David. I wish you the best for the rest of your life. If, in the future, you want to become friends, I would welcome that. You deserve all the happiness that I hope comes your way. Goodbye."

"With that, we both stood up. I kissed him softly on the forehead, smiled at him, and turned away to come back to you."

Santiago did not say anything for several seconds. He looked at Elisheva. She had a smile on her lips but tears in her eyes.

"Elisheva," he said as he stood up and walked across the table to her.

He knelt at her feet and took her hands in his.

"I promise, with all my heart and soul, that I will love you forever and will do everything in my power to make you happy. I would get up on one knee and ask you to marry me, but I don't have a ring."

"The time is not yet right, Jaime. I know you will and when that time comes, I will gladly accept because I also know that I will love you for the rest of my life. But first, we have work to do. Tell me about your day."

He went to the desk where he had been working and brought all his notes back.

"I remembered that Professor Berry was from Antakya, Turkey and that he was going to courier the codex to the Bishop there. I think you should call Johan and see if and when that is going to happen. Then I've learned that we can both apply and receive an evisa applying online. We don't need a lot of information other than our passport number, maybe. We can even pay for it online. We can fly direct from JFK to Istanbul, and then from Istanbul to Antakya. We can also fly directly from Istanbul into Prague. Again, Americans that are going to be in the country for less than ninety days don't need a visa. We can also fly directly from Prague to JFK here in New York for what I was surprised to learn is a reasonable fee. I'm guessing for about two thousand American dollars we can fly from New York to Istanbul to Antakya to Istanbul to Prague to JFK. Plus, or minus a few dollars. Wait, there's more. We can apply for an international driver's license online to the American Automobile Association. All we need is a valid copy of our driver's license, a photo ID and pay the fee. We can get one each for more than a year. I recommend two years; it doesn't cost that much. Also, we can purchase global insurance here in New York and also at a rental car agency in Europe. How am I doing so far?"

"Great! I'm going to call Jonah Weisenberg right now. There's a three-hour time difference so I'll call him at home."

She picked up her phone and dialed.

"Hello," a young voice on the other end answered.

"Hello, my name is Elisheva Gurwitz. May I speak to Doctor Weisenberg, please."

"Yes ma'am. Please hold."

They both could hear the young girl calling out.

"Daddy, there's a woman who wants to talk to you."

"Hello, this is Jonah." A strong masculine voice answered.

"Doctor Weisenberg, this is Elisheva Gurwitz."

"Elisheva! It is good to hear from you. I know you are calling me about something important. What can I do for you."

"Yes, thank you. Can you tell me if Professor Berry has left to courier the codex to the Bishop in Antakaya yet?"

"Yes. He left two days ago and should have just arrived in Antakya today or late yesterday. He probably won't see the bishop to deliver it until today. Why do you ask?"

"Because we, that is Jaime, you remember him, and I would very much like to travel to Antakya and see the Bishop and the place where the codex was actually discovered."

"I totally understand. I also believe that Professor Berry will also. I can't speak to how the bishop will react. Get a pencil and paper and I will give you the Professor's number."

"I'm ready."

"Plus, ninety. That is the plus sign and the number 90 312 1234 567."

She read the number back.

"Yes. That is correct. All of Turkey's telephone numbers are designated under the National Numbering plan of 2018, created by the information and Communication Technologies Authority of the Turkish government."

"Thank you very much, Doctor Weisenberg."

"I am very excited for both you and Santiago. I know the Professor will be delighted to know that you are coming to his town. Like I said, I can't speak for the bishop. Have you read the book I strongly suggested you should?"

"Yes, we both have, and we have discussed it and studied it at great length."

"Then you should be well prepared and know to be discreet when you are not only in Turkey but especially in Antakya. I know you will be successful in your quest. Goodbye and Godspeed."

When Elisheva terminated the call she asked Santiago, "Did you hear what he said?"

"Yes, most of it. Right now, it's a little after eight thirty so in Antakya it would be a little after three a.m. in the morning. We'd better set the alarm for four or five a.m. tomorrow so we can call the Professor at a reasonable time. He will probably either be in the process of turning over the codex to the bishop or will probably only recently had completed it. Do you think we should go to bed early?"

"No way! I think we should start working on getting our evisa to Turkey, then book flight reservations on the Turkish airline from JFK to Istanbul than from Istanbul to Antakya."

"What happens if the Professor is not happy we're coming?" He asked.

"That's a risk we'll have to take. Besides, we're going whether he likes it or not. Don't you agree?"

He looked at her and smiled.

"I should have known better than to ask. I agree. Let's get started."

CHAPTER NINE

—⁓◦⟲◦⟳◦⟲◦⁓—

Bugünün isini yarina birakma (Don't leave today's work for tomorrow) Turkish proverb.

By eleven p.m. they had booked a flight on the Turkish national airlines from JFK to Istanbul departing at 9:55 p.m. on October 30 and arriving in Istanbul at 7:45 a.m. Istanbul time. They would then take a flight from Istanbul to Antakya, departing 11 a.m. Istanbul time and arriving Antakya at 12:45 p.m. local time. They had also each received their electronic visa to Turkey.

The alarm went off at 3:45 a.m. Elisheva was the first to wake up. She told Santiago to take a shower, but not shave, and she would start a pot of coffee. She would then call Professor Berry about 4 a.m. so that he would receive her call around 11 a.m. local Antakya time.

He lay on his side propped up on one arm and looked at her.

"Last night was wonderful." She smiled leaning over to kiss him gently.

She playfully ran her hand over his hair and then around his beard.

"You look sexy with your beard. It looks like you will have a full dark beard. You should fit right in the Levant."

He smiled as she put her pajamas on and left the room.

He brushed his teeth, took a shower, and looking into the beard he gazed at the three day growth on his face. He smiled at Elisheva's words that his beard made him sexy.

I'll have to learn how to care for a beard, how to trim it and learn what is a good length for it.

He entered the kitchen just as Elisheva was placing a mug of hot steaming coffee at his place at the table. He sat down. She sat down across from him placing her cup of coffee on the table. She dialed Professor Berry's telephone number on her cell phone.

After the second ring they heard the Professor's greeting: "Merhaba, this is Berat Mahlioglku. I see you're calling from America. How can I help you?"

"Professor Berry, this is Elisheva Gurwitz, calling from New York City. How are you?"

"Elisheva! What a surprise! What can I do for you?"

"Professor, Jaime and I are planning to travel from New York to Antakya there where we think you are. I called Jonah Weisenberg last night and he informed us that you had arrived either yesterday or early this morning."

"That is correct. I am delighted that you will be coming to Antakya. You don't have to tell me the reason. I am as thrilled as you are to have been involved with this ancient codex. It is really quite remarkable."

"Have you given it to the bishop?" She asked.

"Yes. It was an extremely moving experience. I spent quite a few hours with the bishop. He wanted to know who the person was responsible for finding it, conserving it and who made the decision for me to bring it to him. I explained everything as I learned from working with Jonah and talking to you. He is very grateful to Father Belinsky and to Schlomo Rosenberg. When I inform him that you will be arriving here, he will be delighted to meet the two of you in person. When do you arrive here in Antakya?"

"We will be arriving in Antakya at 12:45 p.m. local time on October 30."

"I will be waiting at the local airport, there is only one here. I will take you to your hotel when you arrive so you can rest and freshen up. What hotel are you staying at?" He asked.

"We haven't made arrangements yet." Elisheva replied.

"Then don't. You can stay with me. Although my family is here, I live alone in my quarters. I have plenty of room for guests since I host many scholars who come to visit us and look at the documents and icons that we have here."

"Thank you, Professor." She replied. "We are most grateful to you. We will call you from Istanbul to confirm our arrival time and again when we arrive in Antakya."

"Wonderful! I'm looking forward to seeing the two of you again and am especially looking forward to you meeting the bishop. You will find him a most kind and learned man."

"Again, thank you and goodbye until we meet again." Elisheva said.

"Sonia gorusuruz." He replied and hung up.

She terminated the call and asked Santiago: "I was on speaker. Did you hear the Professor?"

"Yes. I've been doing research while you were speaking with him. I've found that today, the Orthodox Church of Antioch has assumed the character of an Arab Eastern Orthodox church based in Damascus, Syria. Listen to this. I just googled if there are Christians living in Damascus.

"There are Christians living either in or around Damascus and even in Aleppo, Homs, Hama or Latakia. The head of the church in Damascus is referred to as the Patriarch. So, I'm assuming that the Patriarch is the head and the bishop is the local leader. What do you think?"

"That sounds reasonable to me. Whatever the case is, the professor said the bishop is looking forward to meeting us. That's good enough for me."

They arrived in Istanbul on schedule and were able to make the connection to Antakya without difficulty. When they arrived at the airport in Antakya, Professor Berry was waiting for them at the baggage claim area. When he saw them, he went over and gave each a hug.

"Elisheva, Jaime, I am so glad you arrived safely! You are probably suffering from jet lag after your long trip. Come, let me help you with your baggage. We will drive to my house and let you freshen up and have a bite to eat. Then we will drive to the church to introduce you to Bishop Ecrin. Technically he is not a bishop but a prelate of the church. We do refer to him as a bishop because he is truly a holy man, as you will see."

They arrived at the professor's house on a busy street in Antakya. After helping them with their baggage, he placed them in separate rooms, he led them into a dining area with several tables.

"Please, sit down. What would you like to drink? I have bottled water, hot tea and even Coca Cola!"

"I would love hot tea, please." Elisheva answered.

"The cola sounds good to me, Professor. Thank you." Santiago replied.

After serving them drinks he returned with two plates of *doner kebab*. It is a delicious dish with beef and lamb served in a traditional pita bread with pockets into which the food was stuffed. It was served with delectable Arborio rice.

Santiago was the first to finish eating.

"Professor, that was absolutely wonderful! I will obviously seek to eat that again wherever our travels take us. Thank you."

"I agree," Elisheva joined in. "I'm stuffed. I would like to save what I haven't been able to eat for later, if you don't mind."

I don't mind at all!" Professor Berry replied. "I will take the dishes to the kitchen. Why don't you two freshen up and when you're ready we will drive to introduce you to the bishop."

When they were ready, they entered the Professor's Fiat. The drive to the church took less than twenty minutes. As Professor Berry parked the car, he gave them a brief description of the church.

"You will see signs in English as well as several other languages that this is known as the Saint Pierre Church of Hatay, which is the official name of Antioch. It is also known as the Grotto of Saint Peter's in Antioch. Remember, that in the earliest days of Christianity people had to meet here in secrecy for fear of being burned as heretics. Bishop Ecrin does not speak fluent English so I will translate. As I mentioned before, he will be delighted to meet you. When I presented him with the codex, he had to sit down and literally cried tears of joy. He also has the same paper copy as you have and also one with notes and references, similar to the ones you also have. He has placed the original in a secret hiding place that only he and I know the location of. He is not yet sure what he will do with the original. He has given me power of attorney to become its keeper in the event that he passes before its final deposition."

"Will he consider either presenting it to the Patriarch or at least advise him of its existence?" Elisheva asked.

"I don't think that will happen." Professor Berry replied. "Eastern orthodoxy is pretty much in line with Roman Catholicism. Remember, we learned that in reading the Lost Gospel that before the Council of Nicaea in 325 A.D there were other Christian beliefs and scriptures. The purpose of the Council was for the emperor Constantine to unite his empire with a common belief. Unfortunately, what prevailed by political vote was what we have come to know as Pauline Christianity. That is what the current theology of the Church is today.

"Before this, there was a tradition that Jesus was a man, a pious and holy man, but not divine. That he was married to Mary Magdalene and had children with her. That the communion service was one of remembrance and not the Pauline tradition of the actual body and blood of Christ. The bishop seeks to keep this historical Jesus history intact and available to those others who seek the truth.

"Remember," Professor Berry continued, "Jesus said:

I tell you, ask and you will receive; seek and you will find; knock and the door will be opened to you. For everyone who asks, receives; and the one seeks, finds; and the one who knocks, the door will be opened. I'm quoting from Luke, 11:9.

"The bishop believes, and I agree with him, that the Creator comes to all peoples through the Holy Spirit. Elisheva would know the holy spirit as Ruach HaKodesh transliterated as ruah ha-qodesh which in the Hebrew bible and Jewish writings mean the spirit of YHWH.

"In summary, the bishop believes that the Creator will reveal himself to those who seek it, and it will vary in detail from person to person. In any event, it is not something to be voted on in a political endeavor to unite an empire by an Emperor."

Chapter Ten

—————∽∾∿⌒∽∾∿⌒∽∾∿—————

A mystery is a divinely revealed truth whose very possibility cannot be rationally conceived before it is revealed and, after revelation, whose inner essence cannot be fully understood by the finite mind.

Saint John Chrysostom wrote that they are called mysteries because what we believe is not the same as what we see; instead, we see one thing and believe another. The mysteries are personal — they are the means whereby God's grace is appropriated to each individual Christian

They drove to the Church and parked in an area designated for clergy only. When they stepped out of the Fiat, both Santiago and Elisheva took photographs with their cell phones at the sign posted next to the parking area.

ST.PIERRE CHURCH St.Pierre (Saint Petrus) Church is accepted "the first cave church in the world" which located on the west of Stauris (Hac) Mountain. In 11th and 12th century AD, the cave turned to as a three nave church after such as column and archway addition. The church is a natural cave which outside walls made from cutted stone. Inside the church, collected water which leaks from the stones was used for baptism for long years. On the ground and each side nave, there are mosaics which was destroyed its big part belong to 4th-5th century. St. Pierre statue where is on the stone altar in the middle, was placed on 1932 year. St.Pierre who was one of the twelve apostle of Jesus, came to Hatay and made his first religious meeting in this cave and has been given 'Christian' name to who believe to Jesus in this Church for the first time. One of the twelve apostle of Jesus, Saint Petrus's real name was Simon. Jesus gave to him 'Petrus' name which

means stone and said, 'my community will be set up over this stone'.
According to the Catholic Church, he is the first Pope and Jesus's heir.
He was killed as crucify by Emperor Nero in Rome on 67 years AD.
He is seen as the first patriarch of Antakya, by east christian tradition.
The widely used name of church is St. Pierre means stone in French
language. St.Pierre Church has been announced by Pope VI. Paul as a
centre of pilgrimage for Christians in 1963.

"Don't be too critical of the English translation, my friends."
Professor Berry said as he began to lead him to where the bishop was
waiting.

They followed the Professor through the entrance of the church and
into one of the transepts. There they entered a room with the massive
wooden door which had been previously opened. They saw Bishop
Ecrin, an elderly man wearing a non-liturgical cassock, a floor length
garment with long sleeves fitted like shirtsleeves. They would later be
informed by the Professor that the general symbolic meaning of the
cassock is an inner renunciation of worldly care and vanity, peace and
quiet of heart, a sign of spiritual peace.

Bishop Ecrin was seated at the head of a large wooden table with
several chairs. He arose when they entered the room. He appeared
to be delighted to have them visit. As they approached him Santiago
noticed that the bishop wore a wedding ring on his right hand. Both
he and Elisheva had been informed by the professor that he was a
widower. His wife had passed almost ten years previously.

As they had been previously briefed by the professor, each cupped
their hands in front, placing their right hand over the left, and turned
the palms to face upward. They then bowed slightly and said: "Father,
bless." Bishop Ecrin made the sign of the cross and traced it on their
palms. As is the custom in the Middle East, Bishop Ecrin exchanged
three kisses with each visitor, including the Professor, symbolizing the
Holy Trinity of Orthodox belief. Then, the bishop extended the back of
his hand and each one kissed it.

After the greeting the bishop said: "Please be seated."

After they were seated, he asked: "You must be Elisheva that I
have heard so much about! Please, accept my eternal gratitude for
helping me to receive this precious codex, one that would have
changed the history of our faith had we been able to keep it without
being burned as heretics. Please, also convey my deepest and

sincere gratitude to your family, the conservator and those who were instrumental in making this happen."

Both Elisheva and Santiago had difficulty understanding the bishop as he spoke, but Professor Berry was translating what he said. The bishop waited patiently for the Professor to quit relaying his words.

He then turned to Santiago.

"I have also heard a great deal about you, my son. Please accept my gratitude for accompanying Elisheva on this journey to a foreign land from your home in America. What you two have done is bestowed upon the world and all of Christendom the opportunity to know the divine revelation of our Creator. The Creator, who is omniscient and a benevolent and loving God, will give each person who seeks the truth the opportunity to do so with each revelation He bestows upon us. We now know, with this most complete Gospel of Mary, that before the emperor Constantine made the decision what faith his empire would unite under, he accepted the arguments of those who believed that the unforgiving version of Pauline Christianity would be the one that the might of the Roman Empire would decree. The decision of one man excluded, on pain of death, the previous and historical scriptures. We know that Mary Magdalene was a Canaanite Priestess who when she met Jesus married him and dedicated her life to his ministry. The New Testament was not written during the ministry of Jesus but afterward. That is why, with the exception of the Gospel of John, which was written by a disciple of Jesus who actually was with him, we say the Gospel according to Mathew, or the Gospel according to Luke or the Gospel according to Mark. We know that the writers of the Synoptic Gospels "were written after Jesus had died. We also know that it was Mary Magdalene that wrote the Gospel of John."

Bishop Ecrin paused while the professor translated or rendered into understandable English the meaning and words of the bishop. Both Santiago and Elisheva were fascinated by the words of the bishop but without the professor's rendering his words into understandable English, they could not have understood the importance of what the holy man was expressing.

The bishop continued when the Professor completed translation.

"In the Bible where it states that Jesus drove out seven demons from Mary Madgalene, that was a metaphor for him teaching and revealing to her the seven cardinal sins of pride, greed, wrath, envy, lust, gluttony and sloth and sharing with her the seven capital virtues of faith, justice, prudence, hope, temperance, fortitude, and charity. Together they joined their lives together when he married her at what the scriptures refer to as the Marriage at Cana."

There was a deep silence. It became apparent that the bishop was becoming tired. He sat back in his chair and said:

"There is so much more to learn. I am an old man and easily become weary. I must say that when I received the codex, the most complete copy to date of the Gospel of Mary, I was energized. I believe I owe you two young people and those who made the decision to share this with not only me but all humanity, with all of Christendom, a great deal of gratitude. This has given us a new hope of finally bringing out the truth to those who will seek it."

Professor Berry informed them: "The Bishop is tired and needs to rest. We will ask for his blessing for your safe future travels."

When they left Saint Pierre Church, they drove to the professor's house.

"What are your plans now?" He asked.

Elisheva answered.

"This has been a remarkable day, one that I will never forget and will always treasure. I believe that Jaime and I need to book passage on the Turkish national airline for Prague."

"Why Prague?" Professor Berry asked.

"We need to visit the shtetl Vasilishok from which my grandparents barely escaped murder by the Germans. That is where the Sefer scroll originated, from the synagogue there. The entire population of the shtetl was murdered by the Germans and the Jewish homes that were not demolished were given over to the local Christian inhabitants. Some time ago, a Jewish group visited the old cemetery and had an iron fence built around it. They then tried to locate the burial sites of the inhabitants. They were working from a document they had obtained from YIVO, the Jewish institute for Jewish studies. Originally located in what was once named Vilne, Poland, is now named Vilnius, Lithuania."

"What does YIVO stand for?" Professor Berry asked.

"YIVO is the abbreviation for the Yiddish Scientific Institute, the Yidisher visnshaftlekher institut. It was originally founded in 1925 by scholars in Berlin and Vilna, Poland. Its mission is to document and study Jewish life in all its aspects, with a special focus on Jews in Eastern Europe and Yiddish language and culture. Most of the actual headstones are broken and many have been used for building materials for other buildings. The visiting group were able to locate most of the burial sites by using a diagram from YIVO and place cement markers to locate the graves.

"I dearly would like to visit that graveyard and learn where my great grandparents and aunts and uncles and cousins are buried. Then I would like to locate the location of the synagogue."

"I understand, Elisheva," he replied. "After you two relax and have something to eat, you can make reservations to return to Istanbul and connect to a flight to Prague. Whenever you are ready, I will drive you to the airport. Just remember, I understand your desire to press on with your journey of discovery but keep in mind you will always be welcomed here in Turkey and especially in Antakya."

CHAPTER ELEVEN

————∿∽⧵⊙⊶⊙⊷⊙⧵∽∿————

I've looked at clouds from both sides now[15] Joni Mitchell

B oth Santiago and Elisheva had packed lightly, bringing only essential clothing and toiletries. Santiago had grown a full beard by this time and looked similar to other Middle Eastern passengers which crowded the busy Istanbul airport.

After they were boarded and seated together on the Turkish Airlines Boeing 737 aircraft Elisheva turned to Santiago and grabbing his hand, said:

"Let's say the traveler's prayer for a safe journey to not only Prague but into the search for my past, the Tefilat HaDerech."

He smiled at her and said: "Yes, pray it and I will follow you."

"May it be Your will, God, our God and the God of our fathers, that You should lead us in peace and direct our steps in peace, and guide us in peace, and support us in peace, and cause us to reach our destination in life, joy, and peace. Save us from every enemy and ambush, from robbers and wild beasts on the trip, and from all kinds of punishments that rage and come to the world. May You confer blessing upon the work of our hands and grant me grace, kindness, and mercy in Your eyes and in the eyes of all who see us, and bestow upon us abundant kindness and hearken to the voice of our prayer, for You hear the prayers of all. Blessed are You God, who hearkens to prayer."

"Amen." He said.

---

[15] Joni Mitchell *"I've Looked At Clouds From Both Sides Now"* Co-author Håkan Hellström, From the Album Joni Mitchell Live Radio Broadcasts, 1966

After two hours of flying in which they both read and napped, the pilot announced over the intercom that the plane had started its descent into Vaclav Havel Airport. The conditions were partly cloudy and the temperature fifty-one degrees Fahrenheit with light rain expected by evening.

"I'm glad you insisted on getting those Eurail passes, Jaime." Elisheva said as she turned to him and smiled.

"Yes, we'll be able to take a train with a sleeper and dining car from Prague all the way to Bialystok. From there we can take a bus to Druskininkai, Lithuania. According to our calculations we can either rent a car there, or perhaps hire a driver, but more probably rent some bicycles. It appears to be only 15 kilometers from Druskininkai to the locations of Vasilishok, or what remains of it."

"Lets focus on using the trains to get us to Bialystok first. From there we can play it by ear depending on the lay of the land." She answered.

It took about twenty minutes to clear customs. From there they took an airport bus to the train station where they were amazed how easy it was to use their Eurail pass. They were impressed with the sleeping accommodations in their car.

"That extra cost for the first class Eurail pass was well worth it. I like this car." Santiago said as they unpacked their suitcases.

"Are you hungry, Jim?" She asked.

"Jim?" He responded. "I think I know why. Jaimie is not a good moniker in this part of Europe. Am I correct?"

"I'm just trying to get both of us used to using that name if we find ourselves in certain situations. Jim may not be a common name in this part of Europe. Jim is much better than Jaimie or Santiago."

"I think I understand. It's like kind of leaving friendly territory and entering what can be a more hostile environment." He answered. "To answer your question, yes, I'm hungry. How about you?"

"Yes. After we're through here let's head to the dining car and see what they have to offer."

When they entered the dining car, they were pleasantly surprised. The menu was in several languages including English with pictures. The meals were reasonably priced, and it was a joy to eat at a table with plates and cutlery. The chefs cooked and prepared their meals on the train. They were not prepackaged and loaded from another source. They both ordered the suggested vepro knedio zelo, the national dish of Czechia. It was a delicious meal of pork roast, knedliky, and sauerkraut. Knedliky turned out to be traditional Czech dumplings which use a dough similar to bread dough. Boiled and sliced, they are served with a variety of Czech dishes. She had hot tea and Santiago ordered a glass of Czech beer.

After they were back in the sleeper Santiago said: "I see you enjoyed the meal. I'm guessing the pork roast was not kosher."

"Jaime, I mean Jim, you know darn well that I am not observant unless, out of respect for my grandparents, I am at their home."

"I know. I was just teasing. I've told you before that I'm not as pious or observant as either my parents and grandmother. But this religious experience we are sharing together has had me thinking quite a bit."

"Let's talk about it tomorrow after we wake up. We'll have plenty of time to discuss it while we watch the country side go by. Why don't you get comfortable and slip into my sleeper with me. You can always move back to yours later if your cramped." She told him with a mischievous smile as she began to disrobe.

CHAPTER TWELVE

⎯⎯᠃ᠬᠣᠥᠥᠥᠥᠥᠥᠥᠥᠥᠥᠥᠥᠥ᠃⎯⎯

Ein Volk, ein Reich und ein Führer
(One people, one empire, and one leader)
Adolf Hitler March 1938 during Anschluß
Österreichs, the annexation of Austria

They sat quietly for a few minutes after a light breakfast at the countryside as it sped past at about sixty miles per hour.

"To continue our discussion from last night, Jim, it got me thinking. We are taught in our American History classes that the fathers of our country were mostly white Anglo Saxon men who believed in a Deist creator who, basically, once he created the world just let it go on according to the natural laws he established. He doesn't interfere in human affairs. Am I correct?"

"Hang on just a second while I google it on my cell phone. This free WiFi offered on the train is great."

After a few minutes of reading, he spoke:

"Many of the founding fathers, Washington, Jefferson, Franklin, Madison, and Monroe were Deists. I quote: Deism is a philosophical belief in human reason as a reliable means of solving social and political problems. The genius of the founding fathers is they understood that Christianity could not only stand on its own but would thrive without being written into the laws and founding documents of the country. Deists believe in a supreme being who created the universe to operate solely by natural laws, and after creation, is absent from the world. This belief in reason over dogma helped guide the founders toward a system of government that respected faiths like Christianity, while purposely isolating both from encroaching one another so as not dilute the overall purpose and objectives of either.

"That is from an organization called The Center for American Progress. Of course, not everyone may agree with its statement. What about you, Elisheva?"

"I pretty much agree with what you read but I disagree with one of the statements."

"And pray tell, my love, what is that. It doesn't surprise me that you wouldn't agree."

"The part about the creator creating the universe and the natural laws that govern it and then is absent from the world. I just didn't buy it. Let me tell you why."

"Go!"

"The creator has to be omniscient. Now I agree that our finite minds can not fully comprehend the omniscience of the creator, but by definition, he knows everything, including what's going on in this little corner of the universe in which we live. At the risk of repeating myself, I believe that because the creator is aware of everything in the universe, including our little corner of it, you can bet that he is aware of what's happening here. Again, as I've said before, the rabbis, priests, imams or other religious leaders would tell us that the creator has a plan for all of us and that we just have to trust in that plan. Again, at the risk of repeating myself, I just don't buy it. I believe that the holy spirit comes to all peoples. That is essentially divine revelation in action. Now how different introspective intellects perceive that revelation depends on the circumstance in which they exist at a certain time. We have already experienced the different interpretation of that divine revelation by listening to the Bishop of Antioch speak about the historical Jesus and Mary Magdalene."

"I pretty much agree with you."

"But what?" Elisheva replied.

"The age old question of why is there evil in the world? If God permits it, does that mean he is unable to prevent it? Or, if God can't prevent it, does that mean he is not all powerful?"

"No! It just means that divine revelation by the holy spirit is interpreted in various ways by introspective intellects depending on their circumstances and background."

"Remind me again by what you mean by introspective intellect."

"Animals, of which we are included, are sentient. That is they are aware of their surroundings. Introspection, at least on this planet, is knowing that you have a complex intellect which includes an ego, and id and a personal subconscious as well as a collective unconscious. It also means that we are aware that this life is only temporary and that we will surely die sooner or later."

"Wow. OK. Let me just sit here awhile and let that idea sink in. In the meantime, I'll think of what we will do once we arrive in Bialystok."

"We still have a couple of hours. Fortunately, we will be able to take a bus from Bialystok to Druskininkai. What do you say we start to slowly pack our stuff up. Then, we can get a light snack in the dining car." She replied.

After they arrived at Bialystok, they were able to take a taxi to the bus station. They bought two tickets to Druskininkai. They had to put one of their luggage into the space under the bus but were able to keep everything else either in their seats or on the overhead rack.

It was late in the afternoon when they arrived in Druskininkai. They were surprised at how large the city was. The were expecting a small village. The population was about twelve thousand souls, and it was the most southern city in Lithuania. The were able to rent a nice room with a king size bed, a kitchenette, a bath with both a shower and a tub for about eighty euros. They booked the room for five days. They were able to rent a small SUV with additional liability insurance for five days with the option of early return. After unpacking their gear and a light supper at the hotel, they ordered a box lunch for two and several bottles of water for their journey to Vasilishok the next day.

CHAPTER THIRTEEN

———⁓ɷⲟⲉⲧⲟ⳿ⲟⲧⳅⲟⲟ⳽⳽———

On the road again[16] Willy Nelson

U sing a 1:25,000 scale map which showed considerable detail, they drove towards the location of where Vasilishok once stood. The road was surprisinly good. It was narrow but paved. Like most rural European roads there was not much room on the shoulders. They did not encounter traffic other than a truck pulling a wagon with what appeared to be farm produce. Santiago drove while Elisheva navigated.

"That should be our destination up ahead. Find an area where we can park. Try to get as close to the iron picket fence surrounding what appears to be the old cemetery."

He did as she directed. They sat in the car for several minutes trying to orient themselves. This was obviously the cemetery. They locked the door to the SUV and walked towards the cemetery. There was a sign on the side which indicated that this was once a cemetery of Jewish residents of Vasilishok and surrounding areas. It had once been a thriving shtetl but had been completely destroyed by the Germans. As they entered the gate they began to look for markers.

"I can't believe how well kept this cemetery appears to be. The grass is not overgrown." Elisheva observed.

"You're right, Ellie," Santiago responded, "I wonder who is keeping it maintained."

Suddenly Elisheva gasped and fell to her knees.

---

[16]   Willie Nelson, *"On the Road Again"* From the Movie "Honeysuckle Rose" 1980, Grammy Award for Best Country Song, American Music Award for Best Country Single

"Look, Jim! Here is a cement slab that indicates Yitzhak Rosenberg written in English. There are also some Hebrew characters, but I can't make out exactly what they mean."

At that moment they heard a voice behind them in the direction of the gate through which they had entered. They turned to see an elderly man. He was slight of build and wore a black hat with a small bill in front. He was dressed in grey trousers and a grey sweater over a plaid shirt.

"Shalom!" He greeted.

"Shalom." They both responded.

"You must be Americans." He said. "I can tell by your accent. You are not the first Americans to visit this cemetery."

"My name is Elisheva. This is my husband, Jim. You are correct. We are Americans. What is your name, Sir?"

"I am Leonard Cohen. You are also correct. I am the keeper here. There have been several groups of Americans visiting here whose ancestors originated from what used to be the shtetl of Vasilishok. If you look beyond the fence, you can see that there are only a few houses left in this village."

"Can I offer you a bottle of water or a snack?" Elisheva asked. Then, perhaps, you could tell us about yourself and how you come to be here."

"No thank you. I have just eaten, and I am not thirsty. Come over here and sit with me on this bench and I will tell you about myself."

After they were seated Leonard spoke.

"When the Germans came with their supporters, they essentially murdered everyone here and they burned down the synagogue that used to be located just beyond the fence to the northwest of where we are. Can you understand me? I have been told by Americans that my English is heavily accented. If you don't understand, please don't hesitate to ask."

"No." Elisheva replied. "Please continue. If I can't understand it we can converse in Yiddish, and I can translate for my husband."

"My father was just a boy when the Germans came. His mother gave him to a Christian woman with whom she was friends with and trusted. Like me, my father was blond and had blue eyes and could easily be mistaken as Christian or even as a so called Aryan. The woman raised him as her son. After the war he returned here with a woman, a Jew, with whom he had met and married. I was born of that marriage and look like my father. Unfortunately, they both passed several years ago. They asked to be cremated so that their graves would not be desecrated. Their names are recorded in one of YIVO's books about this place. I left after they passed and moved to Poland. There I met and married a woman, also a Jew who had been orphaned by the war. She died of consumption before we had children. It was then that I decided to return to Vasilishok. When the first group of Americans came to visit, they hired me to keep the grass trimmed and the grave markers maintained. I receive a stipend which allows me to live comfortably, and I am content to work in this holy place. I live in a small cottage not too far from here."

"Thank you for sharing with us, Leonard. Tell me, I am looking for the grave markers of these people. Can you help me find them?" Elisheva asked.

"Yes. I can show you where most of those names are. There are some on your list that I can't locate. Actually, it was the first and second groups of Americans that did most of the locating and marking."

"Where are the original headstones?" Elisheva asked.

"They were taken and used for construction of other houses here and in some cases to repair the roads."

They spent the next five hours locating most of the names on Elisheva's list. After a short break and lunch which they shared with Leonard, Elisheva asked if they could walk to where the location of the synagogue once stood. She told him the story of the Sefer scroll that her grandparents had rescued and taken to America. Leonard was fascinated by the story of how the scroll was conserved and would be presented to the synagogue in America. Before they left, they both took several photographs of the cemetery, of Leonard, and group pictures of the three of them together using the remote function.

They then walked to where the location of the synagogue once stood. Once there, on what was now a piece of land strewn with broken ruble, Elisheva was overcome with emotion and began to sob. She turned to Santiago for comfort. As he embraced her they heard a masculine voice say in broken English.

"Look. There are some Kikes from America again. Don't you people ever give up?"

A second man of the three said, again in heavily accented broken English.

"Don't think about returning here. We are officially judenrein thanks to Hitler and the SS."

"Go. Leave us in peace!" Leonard demanded. I know who you three are and I will report you to the mayor. I have been given the status of a protected citizen."

"O vey!" One of the men said mockingly."

He began to approach Santiago and Elisheva. Leonard backed off again demanding that they cease, or he would report them to the mayor.

When the three of them approached face to face with Elisheva and Santiago, she quickly kicked the nearest one in the groin causing him to bend over in pain. A second man grabbed her from behind attempting to choke her. She grabbed his fingers and pulling them with a strength not expected by her attacker, broke his fingers. She then turned to face him, grabbed his eyes and stuck her finger in them causing severe damage to one eye. He fell to his knees in severe pain holding his damaged eye.

The third man attempted to grab Santiago from behind, but he rapidly turned and parried the blow with his left arm. Santiago then kicked the man's knee hyperextending it. He then turned and kicked the knee which broke the knee and forced the attacker to the ground in pain.

The first attacker lay on the ground groping his groin in pain. "No more, please!" He cried out in his heavily accented broken English.

"Ellie, are you OK?" He asked helping her to steady herself.

"Yes. Let's get out of here!" She said, visibly shaken.

They left the area and walked towards the parked SUV.

"Leonard, are you OK?" Elisheva asked.

"Yes. You should probably leave. I have not experienced this behavior before. Don't worry about me. I will report these brutes to the mayor. As a Protected Person the local police authorities know me well and will ensure these Nazis won't harm me. No go in peace. Pray for those Jews who once lived here. Their memory will be forever immortalized when your grandparents give their synagogue the Sefer scroll that once was located here. I will pray for your safe journey."

They both hugged him, and Elisheva kissed him on the cheek.

"Thank you Leonard. I will never forget you."

They entered their SUV and departed the remains of the once thriving shtetl Vasilishok. When they arrived in Druskininkai they turned the rental SUV in and walked to their hotel. They informed the desk clerk that there was an emergency in their family back home and they would have to terminate their stay and check out tomorrow morning. The clerk was gracious and advised them that their payment for the unused stay would be refunded to the credit card. The next morning they took a taxi to the bus station and boarded it for the return trip to Bialystok.

Once seated on the moving bus Elisheva turned to Santiago: "I'll be glad when we put some distance between us and Druskininkai. Do you think those thugs will have reported the incident to the local authorities?"

"I don't think so, Ellie. I believe Leonard when he told us that when he reports the incident to the authorities, they will be more interested in the assailants than a couple of American tourists. Druskininkai advertises itself as a spa city and I remember reading from the pamphlets at the hotel that quite a few tourists from all over Europe come here. I'd be surprised if the authorities were not concerned about local thugs beating up tourists. It would be bad for business. You handled yourself well against the thugs."

"I'll be glad when this part of the trip is over." She answered.

"Speaking of the trip, are we going home now?"

"I was thinking. How do you feel about flying from Prague to Tel Aviv. From Tel Aviv we can travel to the area around the Sea of Galilee. I would like to see the area where Jesus met and married the Canaanite Priestess that would become his bride. Once we've traveled that part of the Holy Land, I will be content, and we can return home. If you haven't changed your mind by then, you can formally propose to me, and I will accept!"

"I think that's a great idea! It will be the perfect finish to a most extraordinary trip."

CHAPTER FOURTEEN

—◦◦◦◦◦◦◦—

Aliyah[17]

The train ride from Bialystok to Prague went without incident. There were becoming experienced international travelers and felt comfortable using their Eurail passes. They spent one night in the same hotel they had stayed in upon their arrival from Turkey. That night they booked a flight on El Al airlines to Tel Aviv Ben Gurion airport. The flight was scheduled to depart Prague at 10:00 a.m. and would arrive in Tel Aviv at about 1: 45 p.m. Tel Aviv was one hour ahead of Prague. They would fly on a Boeing 737-800 series aircraft, a reliable and proven aircraft according to the information Santiago had googled on his cell phone.

After takeoff the captain announced over the PA system that they had leveled off at 33,000 feet and the passengers were free to move about the cabin. He advised that when seated to keep the seat belts fastened in the event of unexpected turbulence.

"Are you sleepy?" Elisheva asked him.

"No. I think I will google some information on Mary Magdalene since we're going to where she once lived."

"That's a great idea! I will too. Then, maybe we can compare notes."

After two hours of research Santiago put his cell phone down. He had been taking notes.

---

[17]   Aliyah literally means ascent or rise, but for generations it has been used to mean immigration to Israel. It also means the honor accorded to a worshiper of being called up to read an assigned passage from the Torah (first five books of the Bible).

Elisheva noticed he was through with the cell phone and asked: "What have you found?"

"I came across a book titled: *Under the Banner of Love, Mary Magdalene, Author of the Fourth Gospel.*[18] Written by a woman, Robin Jones. There are some interesting facts in it."

"Read them to me." She requested

"OK. There not in the order of the book which I don't think she listed chronologically. I'll just list them, and we can determine their order and value:

"The Gospel of John is referred to as the Fourth Gospel, although it was written during the life of Jesus. There are several items listed in it that are not found in the three other synoptic gospels, Mark, Luke, and Matthew.

"There are no references in the First century to a town in Galilee called Magdala. There was a First Century town called Magadan. Scholars now think that it was a copyist error during the writing of the King James Version of the New Testament using a Fourth Century book of Holy Places by Eusebius. But, according to Robin Jones, that doesn't make any difference because Mary Magdalene was not from Magdala but was *called* Magdala in the New Testament. Magdala means the *tower.* She quotes Micah[19]:

"As for you, tower of the flock, stronghold of Daughter Zion, the former dominion will be restored to you. Kingship will come to Daughter Jerusalem.

"She quotes a passage which says that*: Mary Magdalene who was called the tower from the earnestness and glow of her faith, was privileged to see the risen Christ first of all before the very apostles".*[20]

"The Fourth Gospel is the only one in which the Marriage at Cana is described. She cites convincing quotes that Cana was the marriage between Jesus and Mary Magdalene.

"It is agreed to by most scholars that the Fourth Gospel, which we know as the Gospel of John, was the only one written during the lifetime of Jesus. I may have said that previously. But I learned from another element of research that even the Catholic Encyclopedia states, and I'll read:

---

[18]   Robin Jones," Under the Banner of Love, Mary Magdalene-Author of the 4th Gospel" (Carelinks,PO Box 152, Menai Central, NSW, 2234, 2013)

[19]   Mic 4:8

[20]   Jerome, Letter CXXVII

"The First Four Books of the New Testament are supplied with titles which, however ancient, do not go back to the respective authors of those writings. It now appears that the ancient titles of the gospels are not traceable to the evangelists themselves.

"That is why, Christians now refer to the synoptic gospels as the gospel according to Luke, or according to Matthew, or according to Mark.

"Yet, there are many scholars which attest that the Gospel of John was written during the life of Jesus.

"I think we both agreed previously that the seven demons that the New Testament says were driven out of Mary Magdalene is a metaphor for Jesus confirming with her about denying the seven cardinal sins of pride, envy, wrath, gluttony, lust sloth and greed. They also accepted and lived the seven cardinal virtues of prudence, justice, temperance, fortitude, faith, hope and charity.

"Robin Jones quotes references which state that Mary Magdalene as the Beloved Disciple was a finished soul. By that she meant the so called seven demons that were cast out of her were replaced by the seven lights of the Menorah which serve as a light to the seven nations of the world.

"What do you think, Ellie?"

Before she could answer the captain came over the intercom to advise that the flight was about thirty minutes from landing at the airport. The current temperature is 72 degrees Fahrenheit, partly cloudy with the possibility of scattered rain showers to the east.

"Jaime, I just googled rental car services and insurance requirements. An American citizen can rent a car by showing his International Driver's license. The will need to scan our passports but do not keep them. There is a Hertz rental car booth located in the arrival area with several more just outside the arrival area. We will need insurance. The Israeli government recommends a kind of comprehensive plan which includes, liability, collision, medical, and medical evacuation. The cost is about $250.00 per person. I recommend we go with a Hertz mid-size rental car for about $33.00 per day. I want to rent it for two weeks to be sure we can get back in time without having to turn it in to rent another car. There are higher rated rental car agencies, but it is the most convenient and the ratings are not that much worse than the best. What do you think."

"I agree, of course. Do you think two weeks is long enough?"

"Yes. We're only going to visit the area, not do an archeological survey or a dig. That way, when we return to Tel Aviv, we can fly directly back home to New York."

After arrival at Ben Gurion Airport they signed a contract at the rental car agency for a midsize sedan with the recommended complete recommended Israeli insurance. They picked up the car and with Santiago driving and Elisheva navigating they started out on what they both believed was the final trip on their journey of discovery.

The distance from Ben Gurion Airport to Tiberias is about ninety-three miles which Elisheva calculated would take about two hours barring any restroom stops. Highway 90 would take them to Tiberias and from there they could continue onto Capernaum, which was about ten miles further. Between Tiberias and Capernaum there was a town named Migdal.

"Migdal means a tower in Hebrew. We already know that Mary Magdalene was not from Migdal, or the tower, but was called *The Tower*. It will still be interesting to see all of these places. We can decide where we want to spend the night when we arrive in the vicinity." She told Santiago.

"Oh my gosh!" She exclaimed. "Listen to this. Migdal today has a population of over twenty six thousand people. There is a tower to north-east, above the town. The village is now called Migdal HaEmek. It was founded in 1953. Prior to that year it was an Arab Palestinian village named al-Mujaydil. It had existed there since as early as 1596. In July 1948, the Arab village was completely destroyed due to aerial bombing during operations conducted by the Golani Brigade forces. The bombing forced the villagers to flee resulting in its depopulation. The current town, Migdal HaEmek was built on the razed ruins."

She stopped speaking for several minutes. Santiago sensed that something was bothering her. He didn't say anything for a few minutes to let her solidify her thoughts.

"Is something bothering you?" He asked.

"Yes! I know the Jews have been mistreated and forced to live under other peoples rule for many, many years. I know that in order to ensure Israel's survival, they had to take drastic measures. But I am not always proud when I hear of such drastic measures. But I understand why Israel had to do these things. Do you, Jaime?"

"I think so." He replied, not completely certain of exactly what she meant but knew she would tell him.

After several minutes of google research on her cell phone she spoke.

"When The Prophet founded Islam in the Seventh century, it expanded rapidly, and many were given the choice to either convert or die by the sword as an infidel. Jews and Christians, who were considered to be people of the book, were given a special status called *ahl al dhimma*, literally people of the pact. They came to be called simply dhimmis. They were allowed to practice their beliefs but were required to pay a special tax, called the *jizya* for the privilege of living in an Islamic country. Of course, they were always regarded as second-class citizens. The pact which I mentioned earlier is called the *Pact of Umar*. It laid out a variety of sumptuary laws, meaning laws whose ostensible purpose is to distinguish non-Muslims from Muslims in social interactions, place limits on non-Muslim behavior, and emphasized the social superiority of Muslims."

"And that's not a good thing?" He asked.

"No. We live in an imperfect world, that's for sure. Israel is the only homeland for the Jews that exist. Israel does not have to treat their Arab citizens and residents harshly. I believe they should be treated with respect."

"Where should we spend the night, Ellie?"

"Probably either in Tiberias or in Capernaum. It doesn't look like we'll be able to go much beyond that. Since the 1967 six-day war Israel took control of the entire Sea of Galilee and the Golan Heights. It doesn't look like we'll be able to visit the area from which Mary Magdalene was born and raised. But at least we will be able to see some of the land that she walked on."

"It seems to me that you've become very close to Mary Magdalene since we started on this trip. Why is that?"

"Remember, when we read the Lost Gospel, she is depicted as a Galilean Phoenician priestess that abandons idolatry after meeting and falling in love with Jesus. Among other items in that book, she has been shown to be the founder of the Church of the Gentiles i.e., the first Apostle to the Uncircumcised. In the Gospel of Philip it states that the Bridal Chamber is the most important ritual of early Christianity.[21]"

"What is the Gospel of Philip." He asked.

"Hold on just a minute, Jaime. I will google it."

After several minutes, she spoke: "the Gospel of Philip defends a tradition that gives Mary Magdalene a special relationship and insight into Jesus's teaching. The text contains fifteen sayings of Jesus. Seven of these sayings are also found in the canonical gospels.[22]"

"What are we going to do about our findings, Ellie? Are we going to write some sort of testament?"

"No! Can you believe the reaction that would occur if we were to publish anything that would be intended for a larger audience. No. For me it is enough to publish a private journal to keep as a memoir of our journey. Don't you agree?"

He didn't answer her for several minutes.

"Ok, the town of Migdal is ahead. I'll take the exit. Why don't you google what hotel accomodations there are that we might like."

"I will. Pull into that gasoline station and I'll do some research while you fill up."

After Santiago had topped off the car with gasoline, he drove into an area where she could complete looking for accommodations.

"OK. I found what we wanted, the Magdala Hotel. It's one of the top-rated ones. It's located near the Sea of Galilee, which I can see from here. It offers a room with reserved parking, a king size bed, a bath and a shower, a coffee maker and other hotel amenities. It's about five minutes or so from here."

They parked the car and registered. They paid for reservations for three days. After they drove to their ground level room, parked and unloaded the car, Elisheva remarked:

"This is nice. Look out the window, Jaime. We can see the Sea of Galilee from here. It's still early. Let's put our stuff away and drive to the seaside. I'd like to park then walk along the beaches."

---

[21]   Much of the Gospel of Philip is dedicated to a discussion of marriage as a sacred mystery, and two passages directly refer to Mary Magdalene and her close relationship with Jesus: There were three who always walked with the Lord: Mary, his mother, and her sister, and Magdalene, the one who was called his companion.

[22]   Gospel of Philip. (2023, August 25). In Wikipedia. https://en.wikipedia.org/wiki/Gospel_of_Philip

Santiago picked up a brochure from the desk in the room.

"It says here that Migdal has a shoreline on the Sea of Galilee, including the Tamar, Ilanot, and Arbel beaches. Grab one of those large towels for each of us in the bathroom and we'll drive there now."

"Why the towels?"

"Ellie, we didn't come to the Sea of Galilee to not at least get our feet wet!"

After they parked at a municipal lot, they walked along the beach for about fifty yards before they found an isolated place near the water. Santiago had brought a large, light weight tarpaulin and spread it on the sand. They sat down together and quietly admired the view of the Sea of Galilee for several minutes. They were facing east, and the late afternoon sun was at their back.

Elisheva stood up, removed her shoes and socks and pulled her skirt above her knees.

"Are you coming?" She asked.

"Wow! You have a pair of beautiful legs!"

She smiled at him while turning and walking towards the water. He immediately removed his shoes and socks and rolling his trousers up as high as he could, followed her to the water's edge. They were surprised at the temperature of the water.

"I thought it would be colder than this." She observed while walking to a depth up to her knees. "Look, there is a flock of ducks swimming with their chicks."

"I see them." He answered. At one time there were many other species of birds, but I don't see too many now."

"I see some small yellow crabs scampering along the beach and disappearing into holes." She replied.

They walked for about twenty minutes towards Capernaum before deciding to turn back and return to the hotel. After they showered and changed clothes, they dined in the surprisingly superb restaurant. The menu was elaborate with many starters and main courses to choose from varying from vegetarian to sea bass to lamb to falafel. After dinner they returned to their room to plan the next day and to relax. After several minutes Elisheva looked at him.

"Jaime, as we were about to enter Migdal you asked me if I would publish a journal of our experience and I gave you a definite NO! You didn't answer me when I asked if you agreed. I know you well enough now to know that you are thinking of publishing some kind of paper to document our trip. Am I correct?"

"Look, I know that such a document, stating the facts that we've uncovered both through our research and with the sacred codex, would be widely negated by not only by the Roman Catholic Church, but the Eastern Orthodox Church, and the Russian Orthodox Church. I have not even begun to list the Protestant Churches throughout the world. But look at the positive side. No one is going to burn us at the stake for heresy, at least not back home in the United States. I'm not too sure about here in the Middle East including Turkey. Look at what we were told by Bishop Ecrin in Antakya.

"I believe, and I think you will agree, that there is ample documentation that there was a historical Jesus before a powerful Emperor Constantine decided to favor one Christian tradition and belief over many others that were older and preceded what we've come to know as Pauline Christianity. The bottom line is that the only reason one Christian belief prevailed over the other is through the political power of the Roman Empire. In the final analyses, I like what Saint John Chrysostom wrote that they are called mysteries because what we believe is different from what we see; instead, we see one thing and believe another. The mysteries are personal — they are the means whereby God's grace is appropriated to each individual Christian. That makes sense to me."

He paused for several minutes to see if she had any comment. She did not say anything other than: "Go on, Jaime, you are on a roll!"

"Saint John Chrysostom is an interesting figure. He was the Bishop of Antioch from A.D 386 to A.D 398. He was a powerful speaker and as a result he prevented retribution against the citizens of Antioch who had disrespected the sacred images of the emperors. He encountered much disfavor by denouncing the extravagance of those clerics and lay people who subjected themselves to an extravagant lifestyle in the Emperors' court. He was exiled and scorned. Once again, it proves to me that politics and superstition prevail in the organized hierarchical church.

"When I was growing up in Tucson, I would often attend Mass at Saint Cyril of Alexander Catholic Church. The Pastor was a devout Priest of the Carmelite order who had an inclusive and successful parish which welcome many different ethnic groups. The church would have masses in English, Spanish, Polish and in some African tongues. They also hosted many social events like weddings, baptisms, confirmations and other activities. It was an inclusive church where all the parishioners shared a common sense of fellowship.

"But when I did some research on the church, I learned that Saint Cyril of Alexander committed what today would be crimes against humanity at worst, and antisemitism at best. He was born the nephew of the Patriarch of Alexandria, Theophilus. On October 15 Theophilus died and Cyril became Patriarch of Alexandria after a riot between his 'supporters and those of a rival for Patriarch. Cyril's influence and power placed him in conflict with the civil government, and the city's pagan, Jewish and Christian inhabitants. He gained further notoriety in the expulsion of the Jews from Alexandria. All this is printed on the bulletin of the Church!

"There was a conflict between Saint Cyril and Saint Chrysostom in which each attempted to cast dispersion on the other. Who prevailed was determined by how many more supporters one had over the other. They squabble about many things including interpretations of church doctrine.

"This points out vividly to me that the church is an organization of men who struggle against each other to determine what doctrine of the faith will prevail. In the end, only the Creator is infallible, and he unveils his divine revelation to people in different ways.

"I may not change the way I believe but I agree with Bishop Ecrin that Pauline Christianity was decided by the power of the Roman Emperor. He has no more claim to infallibility than anyone else.

"So, the short answer is yes. I am considering publishing some type of memoir of our journey, both spiritual and actual."

The next morning they packed their backpacks with high energy snacks and water and set off walking towards the northeast from their hotel. The weather was pleasant with a slight breeze blowing from the east off the water of the Sea of Galilee. As they trekked through the historic terrain they could both imagine the events that had occurred in the distant past and the people who walked the same land. After about 30 minutes of walking they came upon the small community of Ginosar in which the Church of the Beatitudes is located. The biblical name of Ginosar is Gennesaret, which in the New Testament is where the Mount of the Beatitudes was located.[23]

---

[23]   Matt 5:3-12

"Although I am a Jew by birth, nature, and soul, I've always admired the words of the Beatitudes." Elisheva said.

"Ginosar is a kibbutz founded in 1937 to protect this part of what is now Israel from an uprising of the Palestinians." Elisheva advised after googling the history of the small town on her cell phone. "Now it's main source of income is tourism."

She stopped walking and turned to Santiago:

"Look, we can plant an Olive tree here in Ginosar, a sapling, for about 250.00 American dollars! Jaime let's do this. Both of our names will be inscribed on a wall of honor recognizing our action. Remember, some of these olive trees live to a ripe old age."

"I like the idea. What names will we use?"

"Santiago Valencia and Elisheva Gurwitz."

"OK How do we do it?"

"Some of the people actually plant the tree in person. However, it takes some time to process. We could pay online, and someone will plant the sapling for us and send us a photo of both the tree and our names on the wall of honor."

"We'll do it when we return to the hotel tonight. I really like your idea, Ellie."

"Let's find a shady spot where we can sit and have lunch." She spoke.

While they were eating, Santiago looked to the southeast. What is that tall peak over there, Ellie?"

She looked in the direction he pointed. She spent a minute or so on her cell phone and replied: "That is Mount Arbel. From the peak you can get a perfect view of the Sea of Galilee and surrounding areas. It says that if we drive through the park, we can make a flat ten-minute walk to the peak. That would be a perfect end to our day, Jaime. I want to do it."

"So do I." He agreed.

They returned to the hotel at 2 p.m. They spent the next 45 minutes arranging to sponsor an Olive tree sapling to be planted in their names and recognized on the wall of honor.

"Are you ready to go to Mount Arbel?" She asked eagerly.

"Absolutely. Vamonos!"

The drive of ten miles took a little over 15 minutes via route 90. It was a scenic drive which took them southeast and then northeast to the park. The entrance fee was 18 NIS or about five dollars US.

After parking they took the improved trail which was flat and only took about 10 minutes to reach the peak. The wide swath of the Sea of Galilee and countryside that was within their sight was breathtaking. They sat together both enjoying the spectacular view that was before them. After several minutes of silence, Santiago spoke:

"Ellie, I understand!"

CHAPTER FIFTEEN

———~wwoσℂⁿⓄⓈⓀⒺↄoⁿw———

*Epiphany (a usually sudden manifestation or perception of the
essential nature or meaning of something: an intuitive grasp of reality
through something (such as an event) usually simple and striking.*

"What is it you understand? It seems as if you've just realized something." She asked.

"Yes! I've had an epiphany, a sudden realization of something that has been stewing in my mind. I've probably been doing this in my subconscious during all these discussions we've been having about Mary Magdalene.

"You always say *bear with me* when you're in the process of formulating your thoughts. So, bear with me, Ellie while I look up the passage I need on my cellphone.

"Here it is! He spoke:

"Now there stood by the cross of Jesus His mother and His mother's sister Mary the wife of Clopas (Cleophas), and Mary Magdalene. When Jesus therefore saw His mother, and the disciple whom He loved standing by (of those he just referred to), He said to His mother, "Woman, behold your Son!" Then He said to the disciple, "Behold your mother!" And from that hour that disciple took her to their own." John 19:25-27"[24]

"Also, listen to this:

"When Jesus therefore saw His mother, and the disciple whom He loved standing by He said to His mother, "Woman, behold your son!" Then He said to the disciple, "Behold your mother!" The word 'therefore' means 'these things being so'. Jesus observed those present,

---

[24]   Robin Jones," Under the Banner of Love, Mary Magdalene-Author of the 4th Gospel" (Carelinks,PO Box 152, Menai Central, NSW, 2234, 2013, 32)

and spoke to them. He wasn't referring to the beloved disciple as a son, He saw His mother and said to her "Woman behold your Son"- speaking of Himself. This was His hour, the time to die for 'the disciple He loved' - the absolute climax of His mission."[25]

Elisheva was fascinated as Santiago continued to speak.

"Jesus was talking about Himself. He was the SON ON THE CROSS. "Then" Jesus looked at the disciple He loved and said, "behold your mother". BEHOLD YOUR MOTHER Mary was not the real mother of the beloved disciple, she became their mother in a symbolic sense, she was the second Eve, the 'Mother of all Living'- the 'Mother' of all 'Beloved Disciples'.Because Jesus laid down His life for the Beloved Disciple, the Beloved Disciple at the cross laid down their life for the mother of Jesus."[26]

"WAS JOHN REALLY AT THE CROSS? It seems likely that the Romans and Jews were less concerned about a group of women at the cross than a group of men. It seems highly unlikely that a lone male disciple would be amongst them when it's not mentioned in the other gospels, and we are told that the male disciples had fled earlier. Peter later followed at a distance to the courtyard, but there is no record in the other gospels of John doing the same. "Then all the disciples forsook him and fled." Matt. 26:56 "And He took Peter, James, and John with Him Mark 14:33 ... "Then all the disciples deserted him and fled." Mark 14:50 - John was amongst those who fled. For Mark and Matthew to say that 'all the disciples fled' means they are equating disciples with men. We know that it was the women disciples who stayed at the cross. John's gospel doesn't say the disciples all fled. One disciple accompanied Jesus to see Caiaphas. Three female disciples were present at the cross. The other gospels would surely have mentioned John at the cross if he had been there. The Fourth Gospel doesn't separate 'disciples' and 'women' The word 'women' doesn't occur in the Fourth Gospel – 'disciples' includes women."[27]

"That was amazing, Jaime. It almost seems to me to be a kind of divine inspiration, inspired by the holiness of this land to both Christians and Jews. It certainly is a holy land to this Jew. What do

---

[25]   Ibid. 36

[26]   Ibid. 34

[27]   ibid. 40

you think? We've finished our journey on this note. It's time to return home."

"I agree. I believe you're right. Let's return to the hotel, pack, get a good night's rest and then prepare for returning home to New York."

CHAPTER SIXTEEN

—⁓∽◦୧ଔ◦ଔ୨◦∼⁓—

*Homeward bound, I wish I was homeward bound,
Home where my thought's escapin', Home where my
music's playin', Home where my love lies waitin'*[28]

The next day they checked out of the hotel and drove back to Ben
Gurion Airport. They had previously booked a flight to New York
City on El Al Airlines. The trip was a little over two hours which
included topping off the car with gasoline. Booking a flight was easy.
The cost was 450 dollars US apiece. The flight to JFK Airport would
take a little less than 12 hours nonstop.

After takeoff they decided to sit quietly and gather their thoughts.
Elisheva was seated next to a window and Santiago sat next to her.
There was a middle-aged woman sitting next to him on the aisle. She
experienced some trouble in adjusting her seatbelt and was grateful
after Santiago assisted her.

Santiago closed his eyes and began to organize his thoughts. One
of the first items that came to his mind was to purchase an engagement
ring and to propose formally to Elisheva. He smiled at the thought and
turned to look at her. Her seat was back, and her eyes were closed but
she was obviously not asleep. He didn't disturb her. After they were
served their meals, she excused herself to use the restroom. When she
returned she turned to Santiago.

"I've been doing a little research, Jaime, and I have a favor to
ask you."

"Anything you wish, Ellie. Tell me."

---

[28] Simon, Paul, Garfunkel, Art, Homeward Bound, Columbia, 1966

"I have discovered something that is extremely interesting to me, and I am following my woman's intuition. I would like to order you to have a DNA test. Would you take it?"

"That's a great question. Are you worried about blood compatibility?"

"No. I saw on your Navy Reserve ID card that you are "O positive". That is also my blood type. However, since my father had late onset Tays-Sachs syndrome, I would have to ensure that I am not a carrier before we start our family. The reason I asked the question is because I've been doing some research on the name Valencia. Listen to what I've discovered.

"Think back to when the Romans conquered the Jews in the Province of Judea in 79 CE. At that time much of the Jewish population was sent into exile throughout the Roman Empire, including many to the Iberian Peninsula. Then, the Moors conquered all of what today is Spain until they were driven out by the Spanish in January of 1492. At that time there were some 750,000 Jews living there. After that came the Edict of Expulsion, called the Alhambra decree. Jews either had to convert to Catholicism or were expelled from the country. Many of the Jews who converted did so to stay in Spain, but many of them continued to practice their Jewish faith. Those Jews were called *conversos,* or *new Christian's* by the Spanish, or *anusim,* in Hebrew, which means *the coerced.*

"OK, Jaime, bear with me. I'm about to get to the point. The name Valencia is one of many that Jewish people is Spain and Portugal used as their surnames. It so happens that many of the conversos, or anusim, from Valencia took that name as their surname. If you were to take the DNA test to determine your ethnicity, I am willing to bet that you would have some Jewish blood! What do you think about that?"

"You know, Elisheva, I have learned to trust your instincts, or woman's intuition, or whatever it's called. I have a feeling that you might just be correct."

"What do you think your parent's would think? What would your grandmother think?"

"I think they would accept it. I don't think it would make a difference or a change in their life. They're devout Catholics."

"What about you? What would you think if you found out that you have Jewish blood? I'm willing to bet it would be Sephardic blood.

There is a term for those people who have Sephardic blood. The term is *Bnai Anusim*."

"At this point in my life, I would feel comfortable with that knowledge. Actually, I would be proud."

"Do you think you would convert to Judaism? Don't answer right now. There is a process invoved in the conversion process. Let that question remain on your mind."

"OK. I'll take you up on that offer. I'll let the question remain on my mind."

He smiled as he looked at her.

"OK, what else is on your mind?"

"I'm anxious to return home and to start the rest of our life and our family."

EPILOGUE

A través de los años: in the changing of the years

Santiago's parents felt honored to be part of the crypto Jewish history, "After all Jesus and Mary were Jewish," they claimed, "as was Joseph and some of the Apostles." They researched and found that many of the traditions in the Catholic Mass were based on Jewish tradition, such as the breaking of bread, the blessing of wine, the altar and several other rituals. Thus they became even more pious and devout Catholics.

They were also very proud of their children and grandchildren and the paths in which their lives were going.

Santiago and Elisheva Valencia watched eagerly as their son, James Morris Valencia, handsome and replendent in his dress white navy uniform, complete with sword, received his commission as Ensign in the United States Navy. His twenty one year old sister Esther,who had flown down from Northern Arizona University at Flagstaff, also admired the older brother she had always looked up to.

James graduated at the top of his class and was chosen to be a platoon commander of the graduating class. He was assigned to begin flight training in Pensacola, Florida as a Naval Aviator.

Esther, too, was an accomplished and proud member of the family. She had just completed her Bachelor of Science degree in bioengineering with a minor in chemistry. After the ceremony the family would be helping her move into a dormitory in New York City near the Mount Sinai Beth Israel Hospital where she was excited to have been accepted to continue her dream.

Their grandmother, Esther Gurwitz now lived in the Brownstone apartment in which Elisheva's mother had previously lived with her parents, Schlomo and Dinah Rosenberg.

Santiago and Elisheva stayed in Tucson as snowbirds in the winter months, but lived in New York and frequently traveled to Israel where both James and Esther made their Birthright Israel trip when they turned 18 years of age. Both attended Hebrew School as children and completed their bar and bat mizvots. They also attended Salpointe Catholic High School which included a rigorous college prep curriculum and a deeper understanding of Catholicism.

Santiago published a journal of that first trip he and Elisheva took to Israel. He described those documents that preceded the writings of the Four Gospels of the New Testament which spoke of the existence of Jesus and indicated that He had been married to Mary Magdalene. With the exception of The White Christian Nationalism Movement it was ignored for the most part.

Threats from this angry White Christian Nationalists caused the Valencia family to take certain precautions, such as installing a home monitoring system, receiving classes in martial arts, and signing up for an intensive shooting course which qualified them to carry a concealed weapon both in Arizona and agreement states.

White Christian nationalism is the dangerous belief that America is – and must remain – a Christian nation founded for its white Christian inhabitants, and that our laws and policies must reflect this premise. Denying the separation of church and state promised by our Constitution, white Christian nationalists oppose equality for people of color, women, LGBTQ people, religious minorities, and the nonreligious.[29]

The children were aware of the persecution of Jews and other religious sects. They respected the experiences of their ancesters and parents but, at their parent's insistence, they pressed on optimistically with their lives and ambitions.

Santiago's parents were proud of their crypto Jewish history but remained pious and devout Catholics. However, some of his more sanctimonious friends stopped conversing with him and one even wrote to the Diocese of Tucson requesting that his journal be indexed as a forbidden document. There was no formal response from the Diocese. One Southern Baptist congregation in Tucson wrote in their newsletter that his journal should be burned. He also received several letters of support from younger people who were searching for a spiritual and religious foundation outside of organized religion.

---

[29]   au.org (American United For Separation of Church And State)

One Buddhist organization in Tucson asked him and Elisheva to give a presentation of his journal and praised him for his determination to seek the truth.

In retrospect, both he and Elisheva agreed that the response to his journal had been mostly underwhelming. They both realized that the response could have been more direct in some parts of the world.

Printed in the United States
by Baker & Taylor Publisher Services